P.C. Tony R
LB 265

"Lima-Bravo One from Lima-Bravo, receiving?"

"Go ahead, Sarge."

"Disturbance, Waveney Court, Chambers Road. Informant a Mr. Clifford Alistair, manager of Eastern Rise Investments, who're located at 3, Waveney Court. A group of individuals – adult males and females – causing a disturbance on the street outside, over."

"Just what I always wanted, Sarge – white collars before breakfast."

Out of the corner of my eye, I saw Feroc smile. He was becoming more like me every day. I blamed the parrot.

"Yes, we all know how you love those rich white boys, two-six-five."

"Lima-Bravo to last contact, identify yourself, please?"

There was the deafening hum of radio silence: no one was stupid enough to volunteer for a bollocking this early in the morning. I gave two quick clicks on the mic – a message to the anonymous commenter that I wasn't hacked off, and, in fact, found their sense of humour spot on.

"Lima-Bravo to all units, a quick reminder to observe correct radio protocol, please."

There was a cacophony of mic clicks as various units acknowledged the request.

"Lima-Bravo from Lima-Bravo One, ETA Chambers Road two minutes, over."

"Received, Lima-Bravo One."

I nodded to Feroc, who hit the lights and sirens. Time to see if we couldn't rid the world of a few parasites before breakfast.

 I loved driving. Loved the fact that my job gave me the right to hit the streets of Lothing at eighty miles an hour plus, if the situation called for it. Loved the feel of the wind ruffling my hair as I drove with the window down.

 Well, okay – in Lothing, eighty miles an hour was a pipe-dream, most of the time, and any breeze ruffling anything would choke you with the exhaust fumes. The spirit of the statement was true, though. And there'd been a few times I'd really been able to let loose.

I stiffened as we turned into Chambers Road, remembering the last major pursuit I'd been in, last year. Remembering how it had ended. Not like I ever got a chance to forget – I had Steve Lassiter's parrot, Idaho, to remind me.

Steve was dead, too; I'd found out two months back that he'd topped himself in prison. He left a note: *Sorry. I'll be too old at the end of this. I was too old before I made my last mistake, really. I just wish I'd seen it. Tell Raglan to keep Idaho happy.*

I'd killed two people – one directly, the other through memories and nightmares, disappointments and abandoned hopes. I pulled the Area car up on the opposite side of the road to Waveney Court, alongside the Marina. I glimpsed Max Rockford's boat in its usual berth as I got out of the car – there were no signs of life on board, though. I turned my gaze to Waveney Court, and wondered, not for the first time in my life, how anyone could function, locked away in an office and strangled by a tie.

I'd grown up in rural Norfolk, the only child of a permanently exhausted, yet kindly and intelligent, farmer, and a woman whose pleasant face was strictly reserved for the outside world.

My life, for sixteen years, had been big skies, muddy fields, hard, physical labour, and the triumph of hope over bitter experience. I'd attended school infrequently, usually when the Truant Officer had come round and moaned at my parents – which resulted in a beating from my mother – but still managed to get a couple of half decent O Levels, and a valuable education in the realities of working life. If my school had such a thing as a careers officer, I'd been absent when they came, but my childhood had taught me that, whatever else I might consider, I should avoid farming. It seemed a lot of peoples' childhoods taught them that, and the government either hadn't noticed, or hadn't cared: it's why Britain was now spending millions importing food. No one wanted to be responsible for producing it at home. Too much risk, not even close to enough reward. A lot of upfront expense, and you could consider it a good year if you broke even. Land was worth more sold for housing than raising livestock or growing crops.

Feroc glanced at me, and inclined his head towards the restless crowd on the opposite pavement. I nodded, and we strolled over, putting on our caps as we walked. The crowd were in motion, but it was the uncertain motion of people out of their comfort zone, who weren't quite sure why they were there, and were beginning to half wish they hadn't come. That usually meant they wouldn't cause trouble – they wanted someone to tell them what to do, and a policeman was a nice, reliable, visible symbol of the kind of authority that can be trusted to know what's best for you.

It was such a quaint notion, I almost wanted to laugh.

Chambers Road was a row of Victorian townhouses that had probably become boarding houses in the fifties, and were now offices. They looked smart – fresh paint, clean blinds at the windows, clearly visible decals denoting names and numbers – and, like the Marina, slightly out of place in Lothing, like an obese man in an upmarket gym. In these socially-aware, ultra-offended days, I strongly suspected a person could get lynched for using an analogy like that, socially-aware types being of a mindset that thinks visual metaphors are worse than the historic and cultural implications of lynching. But I *was* that, if not actually obese, than larger than was usual man at the upmarket gym. At least I was when I remembered that I had an annual membership that made me wince every time I saw it on my bank statement. And when I wasn't knackered. Or didn't have something better to do. And it wasn't raining. If I wasn't allowed to mock myself, then where was any kind of humour to be found in this life?

As we approached the group on the pavement – Feroc from the left, myself from the right – a couple of them turned in my direction. Or in the direction of the foghorn, keening out the blindingly obvious on this grim October day. A woman in beige slacks and a black polo neck stepped away from the crowd, her thick auburn hair a shock of colour against the weather's grey. She glanced at me, smiled, then stepped up to the burgundy door that marked the communal entrance to Waveney Court. I watched her knock, my weight shifting onto the balls of my feet, ready to lunge forward should she do anything that actually constituted a breach of the peace.

I raised my radio.

"Lima-Bravo from two-six-five, receiving, over?"

"Go ahead two-six-five."

"On scene at Waveney Court; there's about fifteen – that's one-five – individuals gathered outside one of the buildings. They're not in the road, and so far, they seem fairly quiet. Show us off watch; we'll keep an eye on them until this Alistair character shows up. I don't want to go kicking doors down with this little lot looking on. Over."

"Received and understood, two-six-five. Let us know when you're back on watch. Over."

"Will do, Sarge."

Out of the corner of my eye, at the far end of the Marina side of the street, just before you reached the bridge, I saw someone waving in the short, jerky movements of a person trying not to attract attention. Moving behind the crowd, I held up my hand, just inside Feroc's line of sight. He turned to look at me, and I inclined my head towards the figure by the bridge, pointed at him, then back at the crowd. He nodded, and I casually drifted back across the road.

The crowd didn't notice. That's the point of the kind of non-verbal communication that Hendon takes great care to drum into the thick skulls of plods like me and Feroc – your oppo knows what you're doing, but Joe Public are well out of the loop.

It also comes in handy when you're planning the kind of rout that senior officers would only get their panties in a twirl if they knew about.

As I crossed in front of the Area car, I flicked my gaze down to the offside wing mirror, which reflected the scene across the road perfectly. Feroc was approaching the auburn haired woman, who'd clearly been poised to hammer on the door again. He had has hand half-raised, the kind of gesture we're taught to use with the middle classes, that means: "I am on your side, absolutely, and I know you have a perfectly legitimate reason for whatever it is you're doing, or about to do, but I do need you to stop and have a bit of a chat with me first, if that's alright?" They always saw that apologetic gesture, the polite, professional smile on our faces. They tended to miss what the working-classes spotted first: our other hand on the handle of our asp, the tactical extending baton we carried within easy, unobtrusive reach on our duty belts.

The middle classes, you see, couldn't begin to imagine anyone doing violence to them. The working-classes expected it the way their managers and politicians expected a little bit of tedious grief from the accounts department, before their inflated expense claims were duly processed.

As I drew level with the man, I saw that he was wearing an expensive suit, cut to deftly hide all trace evidence of a life well-lived, and appetites freely indulged. His shoes, and the watch on his left wrist, whispered money. Even his hair seemed to smirk at me.

He clocked that I wore my own watch on my right wrist, and sneered. I fought down the instinctive blush that had been my response to that sort of judgement since my teenage years, when I'd first had a watch, and after I'd first been caned by a teacher, because "Women wear their watches on their right wrist, Raglan – are you planning to have a sex change?"

Because, you know, a gender-specific watch location makes far more sense than it simply being easier for a left-handed person to fasten a watch strap on their right wrist, and vice versa. I never had figured out where the idea that women wore their watches on their right wrist, and men wore theirs on their left, had come from. And I'd never paid close enough attention to see whether it was true.

"Mr. Alistair?"

"*Clifford*-Alistair, Officer: Alexander Clifford-Alistair. It's hyphenated."

Of course it was.

"My apologies. You reported a disturbance, sir?"

Alexander

I regarded the officer with disdain. I didn't keep a lot of respect for middle-aged police officers who looked their age, and hadn't progressed beyond beat bobby.

I cast a pointed glance in the direction of the mob outside my office.

"I'd rather think that was obvious, wouldn't you, Constable?"

He regarded me with the same look of thinly-veiled contempt that I'd had for him. I flinched – and had a newfound respect for the fact that he'd just taken it.

"I'm surprised you got past them."

"There's a back way – a service entrance. It brings you out at the end of the block. I would have just looked like any other businessman. My clients don't typically actually see me, as a general rule, so, without seeing my face..."

The officer nodded. "What is it you do, exactly? Eastern Rise Investments, isn't it?"

It was my turn to nod, my eyes narrowed. I sensed something was going on, but I couldn't get a grasp on what. "Yes. We manage a series of ethical investment and micro funds on behalf of a variety of clients, from individuals through to company pension schemes."

"Micro funds?"

"We invest our clients' money in the careers of emerging talent. A sort of long-term loan, if you like."

"With interest?"

I smiled. "Naturally."

"And the ethical investments?"

"Typically the green energy sector, and social improvement in the Developing World."

"All sounds very worthy. What's that lot's problem?"

"I have no idea, officer, they turned up this morning and started making a most unseemly racket. Not to mention cluttering up a public thoroughfare."

He regarded me for a long moment, and I suddenly recognised

him.

"It's P.C. Raglan, isn't it? You were shot, last year, weren't you? In the Heart of Darkness?"

He stiffened. "I hardly think that's relevant, sir. You want me to accept that you have no idea why about fifteen people would suddenly all take it into their heads to arrive outside your office?"

"Absolutely not. I arrived at the office at around eight, as is my habit; at about half past eight, I happened to glance out of the window, and I noticed a group of people congregating on the pavement. I didn't think anything of it until the red-haired woman began slamming her fists against the door and shouting. Very unfeminine, but then the women of our Celts often are, don't you find?"

"I couldn't possibly comment, sir. What was the woman shouting about?"

I smiled. "The usual. I was a thief, conning honest, hard-working people. Facile accusations all too often hurled at those of us in financial services, especially in the last few years."

"The last few years since those of you in financial services played a leading role in tanking the economy?"

I felt my smile tighten. "Oh, a class warrior, are we, Constable? I wonder what your new boss, Superintendent Kerrison, thinks to such attitudes?"

"I wouldn't know, sir – he doesn't have much to do with the boots on the ground."

His voice was level and unruffled. I wanted to hit him.

"I expect it's still painful? Your gunshot wound?"

He stepped forward, slowly, deliberately, making his six inch height advantage clear.

"And I expect doing business with a restless and unhappy crowd outside your front door is pretty tough."

"Most of my business is done over the phone or by email. That lot are a nuisance, more than anything else. Speaking of them, when *do* you plan to move them on?"

"My colleague is dealing with them at the moment, sir. What I need from you is a statement of when these people turned up, what happened, what grievance you believe they have against you and your company -"

"As I explained, officer, I have no idea what they feel I've done to wrong them. I have a feeling that's your job, figuring out what the hell's wrong with those lunatics."

The officer smiled languidly. "Actually, sir, that'll be down to CID. They'll be round in due course to take a full statement from you."

"Oh, for heaven's sake! I don't have all day to deal with the police! I've told you all I can – I mean, what do I pay my taxes for?"

"For a uniformed presence to respond to a call expressing concern about an emerging situation, and remain present to ensure no breach of the peace occurs."

"And, apparently, express the opinion that those of us who've pulled ourselves up by our bootstraps and become successful are the lowest of the low."

"I said no such thing, sir. I don't know what gave you the impression that I felt that way."

I attempted to stare him out. It didn't work.

"If you don't mind, officer, I'd rather see your CID officers in my own time. I do have a business to try and run." I glanced across the street. "*If* you ever manage to move that mob on."

"As I said, my colleague is dealing with them."

"What's to deal with? Just tell them to clear off away from my doorway!"

"Not as easy as that, sir." The officer smiled, showing teeth. "We have to take their names and addresses, call friends and family for those who don't have ID with them... After all, if it transpires that a criminal offence has been committed here, we need to know how to get hold of these people again."

"A criminal offence? As opposed to what, officer? What, exactly, do you call what's happening over there?"

"A civil offence, sir. Possibly not even that – it's not illegal to gather in front of a business, after all. If it were, most pubs would go out of business in a week. Sir."

I had a feeling I was going to start taking a dislike to this policeman. In fact, I had a feeling the dislike had already taken root.

"So, you're not going to do anything about those...people?"

"Once we have their details, we'll ask them to move along, sir. But not before that. We have our job to do, boxes to tick. I'm sure you're familiar with paperwork, administration, that sort of thing?"

"Officer, you are trying my patience."

"I do apologise for that, sir." He didn't, to my mind, sound particularly apologetic.

He regarded me as though I were some species of criminal lowlife. I stared back at him, trying to keep my breathing even.

"Look, Constable, I can see you have no respect for successful businessmen -"

"I have the utmost respect for people who work hard, sir. It's when they start attracting attention that I get twitchy – hard work doesn't usually draw a crowd like that."

"Well, why don't you go and move them on, then?" I glanced at my watch, making sure he clocked that it was a Rolex. Genuine, not a cheap knock-off. "Now, I have places to be, people to see. I'm a busy man, officer. I'll drop in and see your CID at around four-thirty. I assume they'll still be about then?"

"I expect so, sir."

"Right. Of course, it might be tomorrow – it depends on my workload." I turned and walked away, conscious of the officer's eyes watching me go. I crossed the bridge, crossed over the road, and doubled back towards the access road to the back of Waveney Court. I needed to collect my car. And I needed to make a phone call.

As I reached the corner of the block, I saw the officer stroll back across the road, casual as you like, heading towards the mob outside my door. He'd *deliberately* not dealt with them until I'd walked away! Well, Kerrison was going to hear about this – I wasn't going to be played for a fool by some overweight, over the hill beat copper.

P.C. Feroc Hanson
LB 599

One of the first things Tony had taught me, when I'd been a complete rookie, was how to identify the ringleaders in a crowd that wasn't yet causing trouble. Basic training teaches you to spot the leaders in a crowd that's already kicked into riot mode, but not in a calmer gathering. As Tony had explained, the calmer gatherings are the places where it's most useful to know who the ringleaders are, because you might just be able to avoid trouble altogether.

Remembering Tony's training, I took a couple of steps towards the crowd outside Waveney Court, approaching along their flank, casually strolling just into the edge of the collective line of sight.

A couple of people glanced over, and the red-head who'd been hammering on the door earlier actually took half a step forward – and then glanced over her shoulder, and stepped back, as another woman stepped forward, head up, shoulders square. I smiled to myself: jackpot.

The woman – clearly the leader of this little gang – was tall, about my own height, with neatly clipped, short hair, that was a rich, deep mahogany. She was dressed in a smokey blue trouser suit, with a deep cobalt blouse beneath, a single teardrop rose pearl on a silver chain at her throat. Her shoes, which looked as though they were probably ankle boots, were the same colour as her hair.

The person in charge of any gathering, however informal, will always approach any interloper. And their movements will always be certain and unhurried.

Her eyes met mine, and held them, coolly appraising, the hint of defiance and challenge in the background.

"Can I take your name, Miss..?"

"Ms. But I prefer simply Brynn. Brynn Ravenswood." She held out a hand. I noticed that her fingers were long and tapered, the nails well-kept but unadorned. "And I'm not exactly 'organising', as such – I didn't bring any of these people here, they all came of their own volition. I just..." she shrugged and gave a rueful half smile " - directed their energies in a constructive fashion once they *were* here."

"And you ensured they *stayed* here?"

She raised an eyebrow. "Well, it doesn't make much of a statement if people keep wandering off, does it?" She tilted her head to one side. "You know, I don't think I've seen your identification."

I held up my warrant card. "P.C. Hanson, Lothing police station."

"Ah, yes. Fear and Lothing in Suffolk." She paused. "Doesn't have quite the same ring to it, does it?" She raised her head, peering over my shoulder. "Ah. I wondered if there was a back way in. Apparently there is – I assume your colleague has been talking to our esteemed Mr. Clifford-Alistair. Let's hope he didn't actually get his name wrong – he gets very tetchy about that, I should imagine."

"I'm sorry?"

"Clifford-Alistair. It's his surname. Hyphenated. His first name's Alexander. Never Alex."

"You seem to know him quite well?"

"A purely business relationship. He did attempt to make more of it, but he's not to my taste. As I informed him, in no uncertain terms." She glanced towards the door of Waveney Court, and stepped forward. I stepped in front of her. "Please don't do that, Ms. Ravenswood. We were getting on so well. I'd hate for things to take a turn towards breach of the peace."

"I wouldn't have thought it was breach of the peace – breach of Alexander Clifford-Alistair's peace, perhaps, but nothing more, surely."

"Do you live locally, Ms. Ravenswood?"

"Locally enough, yes."

"What's 'locally enough', in your estimation?"

"I live in Beccles. Do you want my address?"

"Yes, please."

She gave it, and three separate telephone numbers. "Home, mobile, work. I work in Southwold. I manage the pension fund for an arts centre there."

My brain supplied a possible connection.

"Is that what this is about? Are Eastern Rise Investments connected with your company's pension fund?"

She laughed. "Give the boy a cracker. Yes. Our fund is invested with the imaginatively named " 'Avin' An Art Attack" fund. It supports emerging artists, across a range of disciplines."

Tony was approaching the crowd from behind. Brynn Ravenswood followed my gaze, and a couple of people in the crowd followed hers. The group on the pavement stirred restlessly, a murmur running through them. Brynn turned to face them, and her voice carried across the fog horn and the traffic.

"Leave it. He's gone. There's no sense making a scene, or hunting him through the streets. We're not animals." Her voice was tight with barely restrained anger. Not rage or wild fury, but the calm, quiet, white heat of anger that belongs to someone who knows an injustice has been done.

The kind of anger that is far more dangerous than the more heated, uncontrolled types, because it could be kept back until the time was right – for years, if necessary – and you had no way of knowing how it would eventually find expression.

Wild anger, rage, riot feeling, as Tony called it, was predictable, and, therefore, containable. In humans, the female of the species was more deadly than the male because males tended to be driven by wild fury. Females, on the other hand, held the steady, slow-burning flame of righteous anger. For as long as was necessary.

I took a long, slow breath. "Ms. Ravenswood – do you know why these people are here?"

"Yes."

I was surprised. Most people, even law-abiding people, even people who would never dream of loitering outside some smart offices with intent, were often strangely reluctant to admit anything to the police. People lie to people with clipboards, and to people in uniform.

"A crime has been committed here, officer, and we are interested in seeing the guilty party brought before the formal incarnation of justice, and suitably punished for their transgression. We would like recompense to be made, as part of that punishment, and, like all wronged parties, we should like our voices, our grievances, and our case to be publicly heard."

A couple of men were wandering away from the fringe of the group. Tony stepped in front of them, a smile on his face that always saw people relax, unless they knew him well.

When Tony Raglan smiled like that, or when he was unfailingly polite and perfectly mannered, he was giving you a three second warning to step back from the cliff-edge of hell to pay you were strolling along. I wondered how long it would take the new Superintendent to learn that particular fact. I hoped these men would have enough sense to pick up on the energy that accompanied the smile.

"If you could just wait here a moment, please – I'd like to hear what this lady has to say, and I'd like to see what you think to it. Just chill out, yeah? You never know – you might have something to add to what she says. We're always being given half a story, us coppers. And that makes me feel just a little bit sad, you know?"

I turned my attention back to Brynn Ravenswood. "You were about to report a crime, I believe?"

I glanced over at Tony, who already had his notebook out, the familiar frown on his face. I wondered if Tony was dyslexic, or if reading and writing were simply things that, for one reason or another, he'd been late picking up: his handwriting was terrible, and both reading and writing were activities he undertook slowly, with deep concentration.

I'd never liked to ask him – I'd had enough experience of people resenting the ease with which I approached the written word to know that questioning those for whom it didn't come as naturally as breathing was generally a very bad idea. Even when you were close to them. Perhaps especially when you were close to them.

"Yes, Officer. Theft. Or misappropriation of funds – I expect you'll have all the correct forms and terms back at your police station. Eastern Rise Investments, as you're now aware, if you weren't before, manage funds on behalf of both individual and corporate clients. Or, rather, they *mis*manage them."

There was a murmur of assent from the crowd, slightly louder than Tony was comfortable with from large gatherings of people who had no lawful business being assembled where they were. He drew himself up to his full height – a shade over six feet four – and took a slow, deliberate step forward, one hand resting on the tip of the asp at his waist.

It was enough – it usually was, especially with people who didn't like getting their hands dirty, and weren't used to having contact with the police. The murmur died to a low, restless whisper, which faded to patches of muttered frustration.

Tony stayed where he was, his eyes roving the crowd, his weight shifted forward, his shoulders set. He was ready to lunge if he needed to, ready to run if he needed to – and his hand was still on his asp.

One of the many unteachable skills Tony Raglan had was the ability to sense when the energy of a group changed, a vital second or two before that shift manifested in altered behaviour. He was waiting for whatever it was that clued him in and called him to action – and I was waiting for the slight lifting of his chin that would tell me where to run, and when. Our communication was a wolf pack's communication, small gestures and soft but definite sounds, positions of visible body parts, and something about the eyes.

All coppers were trained to read body language at Hendon. It was a skill that could save your life – but what Tony Raglan could do, did do, went far beyond that training. It was almost as though he was psychic, as though energy was as visible to him as writing was to most other people.

The skill didn't have a name, and it couldn't be taught. You either had it or you didn't. Bill Wyckham claimed to have met just five coppers, including Tony Raglan, who had this skill, in over a quarter of a century on the Force.

I turned my attention back to Brynn Ravenswood, adjusting my stance very slightly so that I could clearly see Tony in my peripheral vision.

"Could you elaborate, please? How, exactly, do you believe

Eastern Rise Investments have misappropriated, or stolen, funds under their control?"

In response, she handed me a plastic wallet containing several sheets of paper, which had been hurriedly stapled together. The staple sat at an awkward angle, and didn't quite grip the papers cleanly. I'd once been fired from an office job for never quite managing to grasp how to avoid similar stapling mishaps.

"I suspect you will find your life somewhat easier if you pass these directly to the relevant specialist department – there's quite a few technical terms in there. It's a little complicated for a lay person, but, essentially, it's an outline of terms for the 'Avin' an Art Attack fund, and the quarterly reports Eastern Rise issue on the fund's performance. We've been with them five years, now – the minimum term is ten years, but we'd intended keeping the fund maintained for the next twenty years – that's when our most senior staff member, in terms of age, rather than position, will become eligible for retirement. Everything was fine, until about six months ago. The rates of return dropped, more significantly than could be explained by normative fluctuations. From which, at any rate, this fund should protect us, as it's not actually linked to the stock market in any way." She handed me a second plastic wallet. "Emails and letters sent to Eastern Rise Investments, and to Alexander Clifford-Alistair directly, asking for an explanation for the dip in performance. All unanswered."

I nodded. "So, you think Mr. Clifford-Alistair has been taking money from this fund for his own purposes?"

She regarded me coolly. "Don't you?"

"I'm not paid to speculate, Madam."

"No – he's too young for that. We like our coppers to be at least thirty before they start thinking."

I hadn't seen Tony move, but he was suddenly standing beside me, glancing at the papers in my hands.

Brynn Ravenswood looked up at him, and something shifted in her eyes. She stepped forward, hands raised in an odd gesture, as though her fingers were describing a square, or a frame.

"You know, you have a striking look about you. I'd like to

photograph you, one day. Against a city backdrop, I think. I can see a painting in my mind – a city skyline, at dusk, a sunset deep as blood, so it looks as though the city beneath is on fire, and you, dominating the foreground, slashes of blue indicating other emergency service vehicles at points throughout the city. The photo would be for reference primarily, but, if I got it right, it could be a work all of its own. Yes...I could do a lot with you."

Tony gave his professional, dangerous smile again. "Thank you, Madam, but I think I'll stick to what I know I'm good at. Doesn't do to go scaring the public."

Brynn Ravenswood smiled. "Oh, I don't know – I think art should scare people, personally."

"Art's like the police," Tony agreed, leisurely. "Comfort the disturbed, and disturb the comfortable."

Banksy. I recognised the quote. I wasn't surprised Tony knew it – we talked a lot about art, when we were alone together, and he knew far more than most people might assume.

Brynn Ravenswood took half a step forward, her demeanour softening.

"And I get the feeling you're in need of being comforted, rather than disturbed, just now, at this point in your life – am I right?"

"What I'm in need of, Madam, is for you and these people here to move along. Go back to your homes, back to your jobs. Mr. Clifford-Alistair isn't here, but he will be talking to our CID officers later today. Everything will be sorted out by the professionals, and we'll be in touch if we need anything further. There's nothing you can do here except get yourselves into trouble. So – move along, please."

Tony had let his voice carry, whilst looking directly at Brynn. People began to drift off, glancing back, muttering among themselves.

Brynn watched the group break up, then turned back to Tony. "I assume you'll want a statement about my allegations?"

"CID will, yes. They'll be in touch."

"I'd rather do it sooner than later – will there be someone in tomorrow? Say, eight o'clock? I can still be at work on time, that way."

"You don't have work today?"

"No. It's Monday. We don't open Mondays. So, tomorrow?"

"Yes, there should be someone in. I'll tell them to expect you."
She smiled, and stepped back. "Thank you. Perhaps I'll see you
tomorrow, P.C -?"

"Raglan. It's P.C. Raglan."

She nodded, a new light coming in to her eyes. "Ah, yes. Tony
Raglan – you were shot, weren't you? Last year? In the Heart of
Darkness?"

Tony didn't respond. "Well, I trust you're coping okay now. Bad
business."

 She walked away, glancing back every so often.

I turned to Tony.

"She fancies you, you know."

"I know." He sounded tired, and slightly annoyed. "I'm gay, not
clueless."

"Would you go for her? If you were straight?"

"I don't know her."

"First appearances, then. She's fit, for sure."

"She's bossy. Needs to be in charge. I don't like that in a woman."

"Tony -"

"What?"

"Are you okay?"

"Yeah. Why wouldn't I be?"

"You just -" I shook my head. "Never mind."

Tony looked at me for a long moment – just looked, Didn't smile,
didn't say anything. Then he turned away, the wind coming in off
the sea and over the Marina ruffling his greying auburn hair, and
lifted his radio.

 "Lima-Bravo from two-six-five receiving over?"

"Go ahead two-six-five"

"Disturbance at Waveney Court resolved peacefully. No cause for
police action. Can you send a note upstairs? Tell CID to expect a
Mr. Alexander Clifford hyphen Alistair at some point today, and a
Ms. Brynn Ravenswood first thing tomorrow? It's in connection

with the Waveney Court business, over."

"Received, two-six-five. I'll see that gets passed on. Can you proceed to Beresford Avenue? Report of a break in at number eighty-seven, that's eight-seven, informant the owner, a Mrs. Angela Dalloway."

"Received, on way, over."

Tony turned to me. "Time for some real coppering. Let's see what Mrs. Dalloway's like."

I grinned. "I'm a little concerned, myself – being a poet and all."

"What?"

"Well the poet in The Hours – he dies."

"And?"

I shook my head. "Never mind. We'll watch the film one day."

"You think Idaho'll like it?"

I got into the passenger seat of the Area car, slammed the door closed. "He'll get over it if he doesn't."

Tony pulled away from the Marina, lights but no sirens, and I noticed the long look he took in the rearview mirror. His ex, Max Rockford, had a boat: I was guessing it was moored here. I wasn't sure how I felt about that – I hadn't quite forgiven the lilies at the hospital last year, after all.

P.C. Tony Raglan
LB 265

Beresford Avenue was less than five minutes' drive from
Chambers Road, and I didn't have much time to think about
anything before we were there, and knocking on the door of
number eighty-seven, Feroc relaying our arrival over the radio.
 Eighty-seven Beresford Avenue was part of a row of smart but
tired terraced houses, built around sixty years ago, and generally
occupied by people who didn't have much money spare after the
bills were paid – "disposable income", for most of Lothing, had
gone out with the fishing fleet. There were still plenty of older
folk who remembered the fishermen's wives waiting on the dock
for the boats to come in and the catch to be counted, ensuring their
husbands and boyfriends didn't have a chance to spend their pay
before the housekeeping was taken care of, the kids clothed, and
what food couldn't be grown or reared at home purchased. There
were still a few who'd *been* fishermen, and fishermen's wives. But
that was long ago, and far away; the predominant occupation in
Lothing was "welfare claimant", closely followed by "retail
assistant." Aspiration and social mobility were pretty much
mythical beasts out here.
 Eighty-seven was three houses up from a corner shop that wasn't
on a corner, and ten down from the Evangelical Church which
doubled as a polling station whenever the Westminster Wonders
decided to trust the electorate with important decisions. Lothing
didn't really have a political cast, beyond "Everything'd be alright
if it weren't for the EU, and foreigners." It was grimly amusing
the number of people for whom "work" was a dirty word who
nonetheless believed that "them immigrants" were "stealing our
jobs."
 Feroc knew freelance writers who'd actually been told, straight
out, that a prospective client "Can get it done cheaper by Eastern
Europeans or Indians off any one of the freelance sites" - and yet,
as he observed, those writers, people who actually had legitimate
cause to be concerned about "foreigners taking their jobs", tended

to be open-minded, tolerant individuals.

Max had been the same: periodically, he'd do a stint of painting and decorating, and had also had the straightforward "There's foreign blokes doing it cheaper", comments. I'd asked him, once, how he dealt with that, and he'd simply shrugged, and said:

"You do it different, or you do it better. There's no point trading on price, because someone's always going to be able to undercut you. If it's not some Eastern European sharing a two-bed flat in a crap area with six other Eastern Europeans, it's a student who still lives at home with Mummy and Daddy, or a woman whose husband brings home the bacon. There's always people who don't need to make as much of a living at something as you do – good luck to them."

It seemed a reasonable attitude to have, and it certainly resulted in fewer "racially-aggravated incident" call outs for us. They were always a pain in the backside, and one of the most likely calls to turn really nasty, and put the copper who'd responded in hospital.

When the door of number eighty-seven was opened, it was to reveal a woman – Angela Dalloway, I guessed – who could have been any age from forty to sixty. She looked tired, resignedly aggrieved, and work-worn. She looked, in short, like a proper working class woman, by which I meant a woman for whom housework wasn't something done in twenty minutes before swanning off to spend the day in the pub until it was time to pick up the kids you resented having from the free day care centre the government so thoughtfully provided, and called a "school", to spend the next few hours screaming at them. People who weren't coppers, nurses, teachers or social workers often think I'm being awfully prejudiced and unfair when I say things like that: the former groups know that's exactly how it is, far too often.

"Well, you got here quick. That's something, these days."

"Mrs. Dalloway?"

"Yes, love. I suppose I ought to ask for your ID, although round here, who's going to pretend to be a copper? There was a bit in the paper, called Beresford Avenue a "rat run" - nonsense. Rats don't run round here, they walk in plain sight with their bloody heads held high."

I fought the urge to smile. I always had a lot of time for women like Angela Dalloway. "P.Cs Tony Raglan and Feroc Hanson, Lothing police station." We both held up our warrant cards. She nodded.

"You're the one who got shot, aren't you?" She regarded me with a flicker of interest. "The rags were going on about you being gay – are you? Not that it matters. You'd best come in, I suppose. Forget I asked that – doesn't make no odds to me. I often wonder how they manage, though, gays – men, in my experience, aren't inclined to stick around."

"I take it Mr. Dalloway didn't, then?"

"You take it right. Not that I'm too bothered about that – waste of space, he was. If he wasn't at work, he was down the pub or the bookies. I'd've been better off without him from the start."

I glanced at Feroc, a look that spoke volumes without saying a word, and we followed Mrs. Dalloway through a living room that was simply yet stylishly decorated, the walls painted in shades of grey, the room furnished in white, with pale blue accents.

My place was the same, straight off the street and into the living room. Only my interior design skills didn't get anywhere near Angela Dalloway's.

"You've a lovely house, Mrs. Dalloway." Feroc commented. She snorted. "It was cheap. And I've done what I can. Do a room a month, every few years, you can just about afford to make a good go of it. God knows when I'll be able to afford decent carpets, though."

I hadn't noticed the carpet: I glanced down. Basic beige, the kind of thick, coarse kind beloved of institutions. I think the nick had the same carpet in "institution grey" - the kind of grey that manages to look as though it's sprouting mould. Angela Dalloway's carpet didn't look that bad.

We left the living room, squeezed through the square foot space bracketed by a staircase to the right, and a row of coathooks to the left.

"In here. He came through the back door. I must have disturbed him when I came back from the shop – I couldn't've been gone more than five minutes, the little blighter." She paused. "I don't know why I'm saying 'he'. You don't hear about women breaking into houses, really, do you?"

It was true: you didn't. Female housebreakers were rarer than successful giant panda matings. Women stole from employers, they shoplifted, sometimes they'd go in for mugging. But they didn't break into, or steal, cars, they didn't deal drugs, and they didn't burgle houses. It was also rare for them to become serial killers, although the jury was out on whether it actually *was* all that rare, or whether, in fact, women were simply better at killing without being caught than men. I knew a female serial killer, and, despite every copper in the country knowing who she was, down to her favourite food – red velvet cupcakes – no one had even come close to catching her in over seven years.

The "second reception room" in estate agent parlance, and "everyday living room", in the reality of the working classes, was as tastefully decorated as the living room, this time in shades of red, with black furniture and purple accents. I was surprised that the reds and purples worked together, but they were flawless.

"In the kitchen."

The kitchen, like my own, was a narrow strip of Friday-afternoon-afterthought, with barely enough counter space to make a basic meal.

Where Feroc and I had shoved a twin tub, Angela Dalloway had plugged in an electric cooker. I looked around, wondering where she'd put her washing machine. She caught me looking, this time.

"I don't have a washing machine. There's not the plumbing for one. I've got a metal trough in the yard I use when the weather's good, or a bucket indoors I use when it's not."

"That must be hard work for you?"

"Not really. Especially not since it's just me. Gordon was always on about how he was going to get a shed, put in a generator, have a washing machine and tumble dryer out there. Never happened – I never expected it to. This is where he got in – silly mare, I'd left the back door key in the lock, hadn't I? I was only popping to the shop – I wasn't gone five minutes. He's had my tin, that had almost a hundred pounds in it. My savings. And he's taken my gin, the little oik. Oh, good – the bugger cut himself."

I stepped up to the back door, with its neatly-shattered pane of glass. There were, indeed, a few blood drops on the glass, and on the linoleum.

"Our forensics officers might be able to get a name just from the blood, if he's been arrested before."

"Well, I hope so. Oh, yes – that was the other strange thing." Angela Dalloway headed back into the room that joined the kitchen, that we'd passed through moments before. "He's had it away with a crystal skull – just a trinket, I doubt it was proper crystal – that was on that bookcase, and all my cards have been mucked up."

I crouched down in front of the bookcase she indicated. The top shelf held several boxed decks of tarot cards, which all seemed to be in order to me.

"How can you tell?"

"Well, he's put the Rider Waite deck on the top – I use the Radiant Waite more often, so that should be on the top. And I don't know where he dragged the Doreen Virtue cards out from – I haven't used them in months. I keep them for fayres, mostly."

"You read professionally, then?"

"Locally, yes. If they don't charge you a fortune for a table." She glanced up at me. "D'you expect it'll be expensive, getting the glass fixed?"

I shook my head. "Don't worry about that. I'll have a word with the glazier, square it up for you."

"Oh, thank you. I would ring my brother, but he'd only go on and on about how I should move away from here, how it's not safe, how I'm clinging on to memories of how it used to be – as if Norwich doesn't know the meaning of crime. I can do without that, thank you very much. If it's not too much, I might be able to afford it myself – fortunately, I do have a bit of money of my own. I do a few shifts a week in the pub round the corner, a bit of office cleaning. I'm used to looking after myself."

"It's only a small pane – I can't see it being much more than twenty, twenty-five, at the most." Meaning, if the glazier tried to swing for more, I'd swing for him. It wouldn't take him more than five minutes to replace the pane, and the glass in the rest of the panels looked like basic stock fare.

I crossed back to the bookcase, and pulled out an evidence bag and a set of gloves. "We won't take your decks, obviously, but I'm going to bag them up and have forensics see if there's any prints on them. Even if he wore gloves, if he bothered to have a look at your decks individually, it means he respects the nature of the cards. He might well have taken off his gloves to pick them up."

Angela Dalloway regarded me with renewed interest. "You're into the cards, yourself, then?"

"I read them sometimes, yes. Mainly, I use runes, though."

She shook her head. "Ooohh, I could never get on with those funny symbols they have."

I smiled. "It"s just a language – like French, or Chinese. Once you've learnt it, you never forget it." My smile broadened. "And runes are a little less sassy than tarot. Well – less *obviously* sassy, at least."

"You get used to that. Besides, I like the female energy of tarot cards. Runes have always seemed male, to me."

"Runes are actually very balanced between masculine and feminine." *Just like tarot cards,* I thought, but didn't say: we weren't supposed to discuss personal topics with members of the public, and we certainly weren't supposed to argue with them over them.

"Hm. Well, at least you can't tell people the cards are saying something they're not."

Oh, you can, Mrs. Dalloway, I thought. Most people were completely clueless when it came to interpreting a full reading. Most people, in fact, didn't even grasp that the Death card usually – though not exclusively – related to change, to the death of unsuitable habits or states of being, rather than physical death. And that's before you even get on to reversed cards and *their* meanings, which can usually only be accurately interpreted as part of a wider reading, I could read energy, and usually found it helpful to bring that in if I had reversed cards, or reversed runes, in a reading I was doing for someone else.

"Is it alright if my colleague has a look upstairs? Make sure nothing's missing from there?"

"I can't think he'd have had time to get up there – I was only gone five minutes."

It had probably been closer to ten, despite the proximity of Mrs. Dalloway's house to the shop. Women tended to forget the people they'd spoken to in shops – including the five minutes spent catching up on local gossip with whoever was on the till. And that's assuming you were able to find what you were looking for straight away, which wasn't always guaranteed. And that there was no one in front of you. I knew from personal experience, in a different street, that the corner shops of Lothing tended to be quite busy, for their size.

"Better safe than sorry," Feroc said, smiling. "If you could just point out your bedroom? My colleague will finish up down here." There was a knock on the door. I smiled. "That'll be forensics. I'll go an let them in."

I watched Angela Dalloway follow Feroc up the stairs, and walked back through the living room to open the front door.

"Tony – alright?"

"Yeah, not so bad. Through the back – came in through the kitchen door. Watch yourself, there's glass." I passed across a couple of evidence bags. "Back door key – left in the lock – and some tarot decks. They'd been moved, and they're the kind of thing that, if you're taking time out of your breaking-and-entering day to have a look at, you're likely to take your gloves off to touch."

"Oh yeah?"

"Yeah...it's... they're sort of sacred, to some people."

"To you?"

"They're tools, to me – but no, I wouldn't handle runes or cards with gloves on. Or without washing my hands, come to that."

I caught the exchange of smirks, and shook my head. "We all have to have our quirks."

"That we do. You don't think they're evidence, though?"

"No. And I know you wouldn't get the okay to take them out of this house."

Claire Harris sighed. "I'll do the cards first – do we think the boxes've been opened?"

"No way."

She looked up. "You seem very certain?"

"Yeah. It's the sacred thing, again – you don't just take out someone else's cards. There are plenty of people who won't even buy second hand decks."

"Superstition. Well, it makes my job easier, at least."

I watched as Harris dusted the boxes. She gave a low whistle.

"Yaaaassss – you were right. Perfect set of dabs on a couple of these boxes. I'll get those lifted – can't tell you when you'll get a match back, if there's one to be had. It's chaos down at the lab."

"So, what's new?"

"Tell me about it. We're getting hassle over three different cases where the prime suspects've had their bail calls extended three times because the forensics weren't back. One of them is purely fingerprints."

"New guidelines, isn't it? We're not meant to be keeping people out on bail."

"Then the Westminster Wonders need to shell out for more resources. More people, more equipment, another lab, ideally. Oh, good – nice little bit of blood trace – Sam, over here. Get that swabbed." Claire grinned. "Here's hoping our boy has an incredibly rare blood group, with, say, three people in Lothing who share it, two of whom happen to be in prison right now."

"Not a chance."

"A girl can dream."

"You alright if we get off?" I'd heard Feroc's steps on the stairs.

"Sure. We don't need you here. You called someone for the door?"

"I'll do that now."

It was a simple matter of a radio call – Lothing had a list of reliable, honest tradesmen, and a couple of women, that we were

happy sending round to the homes of the recently victimised.
 Feroc appeared just as I was finishing the call. "Nothing disturbed up there."

"Good." I introduced Claire Harris and Angela Dalloway. "We'll be heading off now – you might get a visit from CID later." Might – if there'd been similar break ins in the area. Might not, if they thought there wasn't likely to be any glory in it for them.

Angela Dalloway didn't look impressed. "And what'll they do that you haven't? Give me grief about leaving the key in the back lock, I expect. As though I'll be doing *that* again."

She would, of course. It might take a few weeks, or a few months, but she would do it again. People almost always did, once the initial insult had worn off.

 We headed out to the car, and I buzzed the window down as we pulled off. There was something about October air that I couldn't get enough of. I'd been born at the end of October – on Samhain itself, no less – so the month was one of mixed emotions, depending on how long I'd been alive, and how I was feeling about that.

 The air, though, was always beautiful, perfectly pure and harmless.

"You alright?" Feroc sounded worried.

"I'm fine."

"You sure? You're not in pain, at all?"

As had been observed by Joe Public at both this morning's shouts, I'd been shot a little over a year ago. A bullet to the gut, a state of affairs that started with a simple car chase, and a not-so-simple crash. I'd spent weeks in hospital, more weeks on bed rest at home, and a few more tied to a desk on light duties. But I'd healed – physically, at least. Getting shot does things to your head that aren't easily undone and set aside.

 "I'm fine. Just thinking I should probably try and lose a bit of weight."

"Why?"

"Well, if we're going to start seeing guns on the manor, I don't want to present too substantial a target."

I saw the flash of restrained laughter in Feroc's eyes. "Well, if there are going to be guns in play more often, it's technically your duty *not* to lose weight. Maybe even to gain some."
"How'd you work that out, Sherlock?"
"Well, Heathenry commands the protection of kith and kin, of those whom you love – therefore, you have an actual obligation to be big enough for me to hide behind when the shooting starts."
 The one downside to driving is that you can't drive and slap someone.
 No matter how much you might want to.
I glared at Feroc, who was laughing like a kid in the passenger seat.
 "You, " I growled "wait until we get home tonight."

****

 "Lima-Bravo One from Lima-Bravo receiving?"
"Go ahead Sarge."
"Multi-vehicle accident, blocking the roundabout at the intersection of Kellen Way and Marston Road, believed five vehicles involved, no reports on casualties as yet. Ambulance on way. Free to deal, over?"
"Yeah, we'll take that. ETA fifteen minutes, over."
"Traffic have been notified, over."
I didn't respond for a moment. I was still driving, still focused on the road, still aware, but, beyond those things, which were as automatic to me as breathing and speaking were to most other people, there was nothing, just a numb terror, a screaming in my head as I remembered the last encounter I'd had with Traffic, the history I had with one of their Sergeants, and the POL-AC from last year.
 Dimly, I heard Feroc acknowledge the last transmission. Dimly, I heard him tell me to pull over. I shook my head.
"Tony – pull over. Now."
Something in his voice made me listen. I stopped the car.
"What? We've got a serious RTA to get to, in case you missed

that."

"Yeah – and you blanked on that. Because Harry Beresford might be attending."

"I can handle Beresford."

"Tony -"

"Let's go to work, yeah?" I started the car and pulled away in the wrong gear, too fast, engine and tyres screaming. Feroc shook his head, and hit the lights and sirens.

We reached Kellen Way in just under eleven minutes. I drive faster, and better, when I'm wound up.

"Raglan." Beresford was there, a figure of everything I hated and feared about the world. I nodded, curtly, and turned away, heading over to the cars at something approaching a jog. I didn't trust myself to stay around and not do something someone else would make me regret.

The Kellen Way roundabout was a mess. From what I could see, it looked like a red Ford Fiesta had lost control and hit a black Ford Mondeo, the Mondeo had been rear-ended by a white Transit van that had been following, and a purple Nissan Micra had hit the van, spinning off, mounting the kerb, and striking a pedestrian. As I came closer, I gave an audible groan: the pedestrian was actually three pedestrians: a woman with a baby in a pushchair, and a toddler. The pushchair was upended – my heart leapt when I heard the unmistakable howl of a distressed infant – if it was crying, it was alive – and the toddler was sitting on the side of the pavement, tears streaming, shrieking sobs, and periodically smacking the outstretched hand of the young woman who lay sprawled across the pavement, her body crumpled in a way that plainly spoke of an impact from the Micra. The blood from the woman's head wound was pooling far too slowly.

The Micra driver was staggering around in the road, despite the efforts of one of Beresford's officers to move her onto the pavement.

"MUUUUUUUMMMMMMMMYYYYYY!!!! WAKE UPPPPPP!!!" Everyone flinched at the toddler's screams. She looked up – a little girl, with wide, bright blue eyes under blonde hair.

"My Mummy won't wake up, Mister Policeman. Make her wake up."

"I think she needs some special doctors to help her wake up, sweetheart. They'll be here soon. Can you tell me your name? I'm Tony."

She took a long, hard sniffle, and stared at me. "Like the tiger from the Frosties?"

I laughed. "Yeah, exactly like that – see, they don't need me to be a tiger all the time, so, when I'm not doing that, I'm a policeman."

"I don't believe you."

"Do you want to hear me roar?"

She nodded. I crouched over, fingers curled into claws, and gave a playful "Rawwwrrrr!" The little girl giggled. I straightened up. "So, I'm Tony – who are you?"

"I'm Alice. Alice Jessica Annabelle Scott. I'm three and a half."

"Really? I liked being three and a half. That was a long time ago, though. You should make the very most of being three and a half, Alice Jessica Annabelle."

She smiled, but it faltered. "Is my mummy going to be okay? I can't be alive if I don't have a mummy, can I?"

"Well, I don't have a mummy that lives with me, and I'm alive."

Her lip trembled. "But you're the tiger. Tigers is different."

"Well, why don't you pick an animal to be, Alice? What's your favourite animal?"

"Rabbits. Like in Wonderland."

"Well then, Alice, you can be a rabbit. How's that?"

She looked uncertain. "But tigers eat rabbits."

I shook my head. "Not this tiger. This tiger is a vegetarian."

She giggled. "Tigers can't be vegetablearins."

"Well, I am. And that's why I'm not going to eat you. Promise."

I saw a group of ambulances approaching. One of them pulled up a few yards back, and a female paramedic hurried over, her colleagues popping up a stretcher and running behind her.

"What've we got?"

"This is Alice Jessica Annabelle Scott. She's a rabbit. That's her mum, and -" I glanced over to the buggy - "do you have a brother or a sister, Alice?"

"My brother. He's called Harry."

"Okay, cool. So, we've got Alice, Harry, and their mum." I turned aside, and lowered my voice. "The mum looks in a bad way."

"Yeah... We'll get her and the kids to Raphael's asap."

"We'll finish up here and swing by once it's all under control here."

She nodded, and I turned away. I didn't want to see the aftermath of a car wreck. I liked being able to sleep without nightmares.

 The driver of the Fiesta was being loaded onto a stretcher, and jog-trotted towards another ambulance, the crew from a third ambulance was heading over to the Mondeo. Paramedics from the fourth ambulance were splitting into two teams, one heading over to the Transit van, where Feroc was talking to the driver, the other coming my way, clearly wanting to check the young woman who'd been driving the Micra over.

 "Oh, god – noooo!" I turned, just in time to see the young woman start to sway. I was beside her in two strides.

"Easy...steady there. You're alright." I caught her in my arms, and took her down with me, drawing her across my body as we fell together. A paramedic was beside us, a foil blanket at the ready.

 "Is she going to die, that lady? Oh, god, and her kids – there was nothing I could do -"

"Shhh. Don't worry about that for the moment, okay?"

"I know I was going too fast – I was late for work – I'm on a final warning, I'm no good with time keeping...I need to ring my boss, I need to explain..."

"We'll give them a ring from the hospital for you, alright? Just let the medics do their job now, yeah?"

"I'm going to get sacked."

"Don't worry about that. What's your name?"

"Kirsty. Kirsty Gallant."

"And where do you live, Kirsty?"

She gave her address, way out in the wilds of Dogbeck, a village about four miles from Lothing.

"Is there anyone you'd like us to contact?"

"My boss – you need to explain to her. Kate Heaton, Andrews Devonshire."

I paused. "That's in Norwich?"

"Yes." She bit her lip. "She's never liked the fact that I live so far out. Keeps going on at me about 'proving my commitment' by moving to the city – but I can't afford to do that. I only get fifteen grand a year. I don't know anyone in the city."

"We'll talk to her. Don't worry, okay?"

The paramedic helped her to her feet as his colleague brought a wheelchair over.

"Let's get you loaded up – give you the once over at the hospital, okay? At least that way you'll get a sick note for your boss."

I walked away, trying to keep my breathing even, trying to quiet the screaming in my head.

"What do you reckon?"

Harry Beresford was suddenly standing in front of me – I had no idea how. I swallowed hard, taking a breath as I gathered my thoughts.

"Well, the Fiesta caused it – speeding?"

Beresford nodded. "Nearly ninety."

"Bloody hell." I closed my eyes, hating what I was about to do to a woman who probably relied on being able to drive the way most people relied on being able to drink clean water, but, at the same time, seeing the broken body of that young mother, hearing the tremulous voice of three-and-a-half-year-old Alice, the screams of her brother, Harry.

"The Micra was speeding, too. The driver admitted it – she was running late for getting to Norwich for work. I clocked the dash as I walked past – eighty three."

Beresford shook his head. "So, prior to impact, probably closer to eighty five. How's the pedestrian?"

It was my turn to shake my head.

"Doesn't look good. She's got two young kids. Alice, she's three and a half, and a baby boy, Harry." I blinked back tears. "Alice just wanted her mum to wake up. I told her I was a tiger. She's a rabbit."

"What the hell have you done, Beresford? Tony? Tony – look at me."

I turned towards the voice. "Feroc." He seemed blurred, somehow, and my eyes were stinging. I blinked hard. Tears. I was blinking back tears. I suddenly felt tired. I just needed to sit down for a second or two, I'd be fine in a minute -

"Tony! Medic – can we get a medic over here?! Harry!"

I heard shouts in the distance, felt the temperature drop. And then everything went away.

"What happened?"

"You blacked out. You'd been crying. Did Beresford say something to you?"

"Beresford?"

"Yeah – Harry Beresford, from Traffic. Did he say something?"

"Harry's Alice's brother. What's happening to their mum, Feroc? Is she going to be okay?"

I stood up – and a wave of dizziness sent me staggering backwards.

"Sit still for a minute, yeah? The doc'll be here soon."

"I'm alright."

"No, you're not. Sit still, and let me take care of you for once."

There was a sharp *swoosh* as the faded curtain around the cubicle was swept aside. A tall, slim Asian doctor came over to the chair I was sitting on, smiling demurely.

"P.C. Raglan? I'm Doctor Ajit Singh. Now, I understand you had some sort of dizziness episode?"

"I don't really remember. I'd been unsettled by an RTA – a woman had been badly injured. She had two little kids. It took me bad, for some reason. I mean, I've seen things like that before..."

"The human body can be very strange sometimes. The mind also. Now, I'm just going to shine a light into your eyes – try not to look away." I forced myself to look into the light. "Hmm. That all seems fine. Can you remove your shirt for me? I need to take your blood pressure."

I complied, feeling as though I was moving through a dreamscape. Even the tightness of the blood pressure cuff didn't seem quite real.

"What's he done now?"

"Had a bit of a flakey moment at an RTA. It's Sonia, isn't it?"

"Yep – Feroc, right? Is this the one with the woman with the two kids?"

I looked up. "How is she?"

"If you could keep still, please?"

Sonia laughed. "I'm surprised he's moving, Ajit. Doesn't usually like to do anything too physical."

Dr. Singh laughed. My voice, when I spoke, was a growl. "I'm right here. How's the woman?"

"She'll pull through, we think." Sonia sounded shaken by the venom in my voice. "Probably going to be paralysed, though. We've managed to track down the husband – he works nights. He's ringing round trying to get a lift in."

"What a mess." I was coming back. I could hear the exhaustion in my voice.

Feroc glanced at me. "I spoke to Wyckham while they were bringing you in. He said you can clock off for the day if you want?"

I shook my head. "I'm not leaving them a unit down. I need to deal with this."

Dr. Singh stepped back, unwrapping the blood pressure cuff. "Well, everything seems to be okay. I think you probably had a stress reaction. These things happen. Your blood pressure is a little high, although that could be to do with your -"

"Don't." I got to my feet, steady now, my vision and focus clear. "Don't even start." I started walking, ready to get back to work. "C'mon, Feroc." Something occurred to me. "Where's the Area Car?"

"Harry Beresford said he'd bring it round to the hospital, wait and see if you were fit to head out again."

I sighed. "Right. Let's get this over with, then."

Sergeant Harry Beresford
Traffic

I watched Feroc and Tony as they came out of the side entrance. Feroc had one hand resting on the small of Tony's back, and was glancing up at him every few steps.

 I got out of the Area car, and leaned against the top of the driver's door.

I hadn't realised, until he'd blacked out at the accident scene on Kellen Way, just how shaken by last year's POL-AC Tony still was, and I felt bad for the hard time I'd given him. I wouldn't even be questioning any of the drivers involved in today's hell, and I knew that they'd be treated better than I'd treated Tony Raglan.

 Yes, he was a copper – but he was human, too. Flawed, the way we all were.

 The way I'd been, over Max Rockford.

"Sarge."

Feroc Hanson stepped forward, his eyes meeting mine, sparking with fury. I stepped back from the car, closed the driver's door softly, and walked round to stand in front of Tony, between him and Feroc.

"You okay to drive?"

"So they say."

"Bad business out there today."

"Yeah."

"They were saying at the scene the Mondeo driver probably isn't going to make it. The Fiesta driver was DoA."

Dead on Arrival. He'd thrown up, then passed out, in the ambulance, and never regained consciousness. Barely nineteen. His mother had had to be sedated when she'd been told, apparently.

"They think the pedestrian who was hit is going to be paralysed. But she should pull through."

I shook my head, and looked away.

"Are you going to get out of my way? Sarge?"

Instead, I held out my hand. "I'm sorry, Tony. I've been a first-class prat, for a second-rate nobody who didn't deserve the attention."

Tony Raglan regarded me for a long moment, then, slowly, extended his own hand.

"His boat's in at the Marina. Means he'll be around at some point."

I shook my head.

"It was never about him. Not really."

"It was about getting one up on me?"

"Yeah. Daft, and unprofessional."

Tony took my hand, finally. "Completely. But we've all done daft things in our time."

I gave a half smile. "Amen to that. Friends?"

"Colleagues. We'll see about friends."

"I'll take that."

We shook hands, then broke off and stepped back, in the awkward way of men who don't know quite what to do with themselves once business is done and dusted, emotions being a sign of weakness, and all that jazz.

Tony opened the driver's door, and paused as he was about to get behind the wheel.

"Give you a lift? Sarge?"

"Yeah, that'd be great. Cheers, Constable."

P.C. Feroc Hanson
LB 599

I couldn't stop thinking about the woman who'd been hit by the Nissan. About her kids. I couldn't believe someone's whole life had been turned upside down by someone else's laziness. Their selfishness.

No one has a "right" to drive – and yet I come across a hell of a lot of people, in the day to day of my job, in casual conversation, online and in the letters page of the local paper, who seem to believe that driving *is* a right, that no one should ever be allowed to interfere with the sovereignty of the Great British Motorist. Sod cyclists. Screw pedestrians. Buses can go to hell. And how *dare* coppers book people for speeding, or using a mobile phone? Don't they have real criminals to catch?

Yes. We do, actually. We don't want to waste our time sorting out your cock ups on the road, or trying to stop you ending up dead in a ditch. But, sometimes, I wonder why we bother. Stop enforcing traffic regulations, stop laying down the law to motorists, and let them kill each other. It probably wouldn't take long.

We live in a digital age – with a bit of co-operation from the business sector, there's no reason most people need a car, anyway. It's an unpopular opinion, but we have to face facts – we can't carry on with everyone simply stating that they "have to have" a car, and thinking it's their right, getting up in arms when circumstances, or their own actions, mean they *can't* have that car.

I glanced across at Tony. He had the same look he always did when he was driving, his gaze fixed on some point in the distance, his hands, on the steering wheel, as light and sure as a potter's at their craft. I could barely tell he was breathing.

In the rearview mirror, I watched Harry Beresford fiddling with his phone. I suspected he was probably dealing with emailed reports of the crash at Kellen Way.

I shook my head. Beresford caught the gesture.

"You'll see a lot worse than that, son."

"I keep thinking about that woman, the pedestrian..." I shook my head. "I hate drivers, some times."

"Thanks." Tony didn't even take his eyes off the road for a second. There was an edge to his voice that stung.

"I didn't mean you."

"But someone died because of me. Two people, if you include Steve. How am I any different?"

"You didn't mean it."

"I doubt they did. The Fiesta driver, alright, he was a young twat, it's easy to blame him. But you know what? I was a young twat once. The only difference between me and that lad is, I didn't kill myself before I got a chance to grow up. And the woman in the Micra? Stars and stones, Feroc – she was late for work. She works for a boss who thinks she's a waste of space because she can't afford to live in the city, or doesn't want to. I've been there, too, Feroc, dealing with people who were just looking for a chance to crap on me because I wasn't interested in what passed for city life. I'm lucky I can drive to work in ten minutes, twenty max, if the traffic on the bridge is bad – but there's been times I haven't lived that close. Times I've been running late."

I shook my head, more aggressively this time. "But work isn't more important than the law. It's not more important than someone's life."

"For some people, it is. For some people, it's *their* life."

"There's always other jobs."

"Not these days, there isn't."

"There is if you look."

"You're lucky, Feroc – you're out of all of that. You're not living in terror of a brown envelope landing on your doormat because some prat in a suit told you no, for no reason other than he didn't like your face, or where you lived, or what kind of deodorant you used. You know if someone gets sacked, it's a minimum – a MINIMUM – of three months before the DWP'll even give them anything? Three months with no money coming in – I couldn't manage."

"Yeah, but -"

"No." Tony's voice was harsh, anger flashing in eyes that never left the road. "People fuck up, Feroc. We fumble around, doing our best, and, sometimes, that best isn't even halfway good enough. The world's a hard place, and it's only getting harder. Especially in Lothing, and places like Lothing. We're protected from a lot of the crap of the world out there, because we belong to the biggest and most powerful gang in town. Imagine, just for a moment, how it must feel to just be you against the world. Imagine how it feels to be that weak. That powerless. That insignificant. Imagine how it feels when no one gives a toss about you, your life, your ambitions, your frustrations, your ideas, your problems."

I didn't respond. I didn't think Tony really got it. It wasn't about life being "hard", it was about people being entitled. Old people thinking they were entitled to free this, free that, to automatic respect, to an easy life, because their childhoods had been hard, and young people thinking they were entitled to be right, to never have to struggle, because they'd been pampered and indulged from day one. They'd had every whim catered to from the day they were born, because businesses thought they were a walking piggy bank.

"Where did you grow up, Feroc?"

I glanced at Tony, startled by the question.

"Cambridge. A couple of miles from the city centre – you know this. We've talked about it before, Tony."

"What did your parents do?"

"My father was a business consultant, my mother was an artist. She ran courses part time, did a lot of voluntary stuff."

"What was your first job?"

"A paper round, when I was thirteen. Because I didn't expect everything to be handed to me on a plate."

"Neither do these kids, Feroc. Most of them, anyway. You got a paper round because you lived in the suburbs, where a paper round was an option, and because you grew up at a time before businesses decided it was cheaper to have a bloke in a van deliver all the papers in a given area, rather than the hassle of three or four kids on bikes. Or before they decided to stop delivering papers at all, because everyone had a motor, so there was no excuse for people not picking up their papers themselves. Before newspapers started the downward spiral to obsolescence, because everyone's getting their news through some kind of screen. You got a paper round at a time paper rounds were a thing, from a position of it not really mattering if you got a job or not. That paper round meant you had someone to vouch for you when you went for other jobs. It meant you had someone who rated you because you'd been useful. That's the only reason most people give a toss about anyone – usefulness. If you can't prove that you can be useful, you might as well give up and off yourself."

We spent the rest of the journey back to Lothing nick in silence. I didn't like the way Tony had made me feel, and I could sense from the shift in his energy that he'd suddenly become angry with me. We dropped Harry Beresford off, and headed back to Kellen Way.

Traffic had mostly cleared the scene; the Micra was being lifted onto a low-loader, behind the Fiesta, when we drove by. They'd be taken to the divisional garage, and Harry Beresford, or someone very like him, would give them a thorough going over. You never knew when some little toerag would get a free pass on driving like a maniac because there was a tiny bit of wear on one of his brake pads.

We pulled in a few yards past the rapidly-clearing accident scene, and sat in a strange kind of silence, watching the last echoes of chaos fade away. Soon, the only sign that anything had happened here would be the blue and white signs one of the Traffic officers were already putting up: POLICE. FATAL ACCIDENT HERE. DID YOU SEE ANYTHING? The concept of minimalism was anathema to the police. As was the idea that we should maybe try and conserve the rainforests. The more paperwork we could generate, the better. You'd never have guessed we were a public sector service, would you?

Tony turned to me. "I think it's about time I laid out a little bit of explanation on how I see the world, and my place in it. You deserve to know what you're signing up for, and, up until now, we haven't really talked about the big stuff. We've just muddled along. Let's find a caff, grab a coffee, okay?"

I had a feeling I didn't really have a choice. As though he were reading my mind, Tony continued;

"Or, y'know, we can carry on as we are, and eventually split up in a hail of bullets because neither of us is the man the other thought he was, and we've hit a fork in the road of relationship, a place where our opinions necessitate us taking opposite paths. It really is entirely up to you." He paused. "I'll pay for the coffee, if it helps."

"I don't want to end up in an argument -"

"Feroc. This won't be an argument. It'll be a discussion. A debate."

"Another word for an argument."

"No." Tony was getting frustrated: his fingers were gripping the steering wheel as though he were imagining it was my neck, and contemplating strangling me. His eyes flashed with something darkly wild, and there was an edge to his voice that genuinely terrified me.

"Stars and stones – discussions and debates *stop* arguments happening. Believe me, I grew up in a house where no one talked about anything, ever, and, every so often, my mother would go batshit crazy. I nearly died because I lived with two people who made a big thing out of how they didn't argue." Tony nearly spat the last two words. He turned his head, but not before I'd caught the fury that twisted his face into something ugly and unrecognisable. He didn't speak for the span of five cars passing. Gulls shrieked in their wide, wild circles overhead.

When he did speak, his voice was low, hoarse, and shot through with pain. And he still didn't look at me. "I won't live like that again, Feroc. If you won't get a coffee with me now, if you won't listen to me while we have time to talk, then I'll drive you to a hotel tonight, once you've got whatever you're likely to need immediately. You can look for your own place, and I'll do you the courtesy of driving the rest of your stuff there."

I stared at him, stunned. "Tony – Tony.... I love you, Tony -"

He turned and looked at me then, and I saw the tears glistening in his eyes. "Then listen to me. Let me explain things you may not like."

I reached out a hand, and touched his shoulder.

"Of course. I'm sorry."

He sighed. "So am I. Because I have a feeling I've hurt you, and that's the last thing I ever wanted to do." He slammed the palm of one hand against the steering wheel. It shocked me as deeply as seeing a shepherd beat a sheepdog puppy would have done. "But I won't live in silence and shame again, Feroc. I won't have you stab me because I do something you don't like, one day. I won't spend the night in a graveyard because I've had to run from you."

"The scar across your stomach - ?"

Tony nodded. "My mother had seen a framed photograph of the guy I was dating at the time. It was stupid of me to have it out, but he'd given it to me as a Yule gift. I'd only meant to have it out for a few minutes, then I was going to lock it away somewhere safe. I fell asleep. She came into my room while I was sleeping, and saw it." His voice was thick and brittle, and with a flash of understanding I realised why he didn't have any photographs at home, why it took him up to an hour, sometimes, of pacing round the house, putting everything, from the mugs we'd used for coffee to the TV remote, away, before he could go to bed. I understood why he woke several times during the night, or the day, if we were working nights, and leapt out of bed, to fling the door open. I understood what I'd been afraid to ask him about – the knife that he always checked was under his pillow before he settled to what passed for sleep with him.

For a long moment – the span of three cars and an articulated lorry passing – I didn't speak. Finally, almost in a whisper, the words came.

"I'll buy the coffee. And I will never, ever, hurt you – no matter who you are, or what you believe."

Tony smiled, and swung the car round as I radioed in that Tony wasn't feeling too good, and I'd like to take Inspector Wyckham up on his offer to put us both out sick.

Sergeant Aimee Gardner
LB 761

"Received, five-nine-nine. Tell Two-six-five we all hope he feels better soon. I'll try and catch you when you drop the car back, over."

Wyckham, who'd popped his head into the CAD room on his way past, raised an enquiring eyebrow. "Tony and Feroc are going sick, Sir. Tony's not feeling too good, apparently."

"I'm not surprised. I was impressed he wanted to head out once he'd dropped Beresford back here, to be honest – he didn't look right then."

"Yeah, what's going on with him and Harry Beresford? Have they kissed and made up, or something? They weren't snarling death threats at each other in the yard earlier – that's not normal."

"And Tony didn't chuck him under a car at Kellen Way. Decidedly not normal. I think you could be right – I think our favourite enemies may have called a truce."

I paused. "Is that a good thing, or a bad thing, Sir?"

Wyckham turned to leave. "I have no idea, Sergeant."

I worried about Tony Raglan, for a very simple reason: if the Force had still been the way it used to be, and I'd been expected to play straight, Tony Raglan was someone I honestly wouldn't have minded playing with, even before his own sexuality became known. He was a steady, reliable kind of guy, with a gentle sense of humour, and a genuine respect for people. He was a good mate, and, if it had come down to it, he would have made an excellent beard.

And, as I'd discovered on a day off, we shared similar interests. There'd been an exhibition from one of the local photography groups, and we'd both ended up there, although I'd taken care to ensure Tony Raglan didn't see me – he'd seemed lost in the work, and I hadn't wanted to shatter whatever spell he was under.

I'd watched him for a while, following him without being noticed. He, like me, was one of those people who actually *looked* at pictures in exhibitions, rather than just prowling round throwing glances at the walls every so often. He would stand in front of a piece, move around it, looking at it from different angles. He would get right up close, and back way, way off. He would look at a selection of work by the same artist as a whole, searching for the pattern that that artist worked to.

 He'd actually bought one of the photographs – a macro close up of an old, rusted anchor, one of several that were laid out on a stretch of clifftop common land. The left hand curve of the anchor framed a small, scruffy dog.

 The choice of that photograph told me a lot about the man that was Tony Raglan, and I wished I had a way to find out more.

 I'd been pleased – if a little surprised – when it all came out about Tony and Feroc. I was glad Tony had someone: blokes didn't really manage on their own, not the way women did. We were trained to coping and looking after ourselves from our earliest girlhood, when our mothers dropped us at the school gates, and walked away with a smile and a wave, but, when our brothers started, would walk them in to the playground, and hover nearby, anxious that their little boys should never have any struggle making new friends. We were invited to "pop into the kitchen and get some juice, if you're thirsty", while our brothers were asked what they wanted, did our mother need to go to the shop for anything, which glass did they want their juice in? As a teenager, I'd been expected to clean my own room, put my laundry on, and collect it once my mother had ironed it, after it had dried on the line stretched across the front balcony. My brothers, on the other hand, had had everything done for them.

 I'd left home at eighteen: both my brothers – thirty and twenty-four – still lived with our mother, although John Joseph, my elder brother, was considering moving in with a girlfriend that things were looking a bit serious with.

 Like I say, blokes don't really manage on their own.

P.C. Feroc Hanson
LB 599

"I'll drive." Tony glanced at me as we headed out of the locker room.

"It's my car."

"I know, but you already look like you're lost in your thoughts and memories. I'd rather not be the next wipeout someone from here's called to."

Tony paled, and, wordlessly, handed me the keys to his Civic. Recovering his composure a little, he grinned. "Try and do the kind of non-fatal damage that means the insurance company'll write it off, yeah? I need something that suits my image better."

I snorted. "What, like a Ferrari?"

"Nah. Too flash. Wouldn't mind a Porsche, though."

"Oh, yeah. Because a Porsche isn't flash."

"Not if you get the right kind of Porsche it's not. Where're we headed, anyway?"

"Home. Since we're signed off sick. We can grab a Chinese on the way."

"Since we're signed off sick, we can grab some beer as well."

"It's going to be that kind of talk, is it?"

"Maybe."

I looked at him – really *looked* at him. The way you do when you'd swear you saw someone's soul. I took in the lines on his face, the slight trace of hair where he hadn't quite shaved close, the flecks of gold in eyes that looked like chocolate slowly melting on a warm day. Tony Raglan inspired lazy metaphors and cliched phrases, somehow – I didn't quite understand why.

 In that moment, I envied the painters. I only had words, and there weren't enough words in my language to write the complexity of the man I loved, or the complexity of why I loved him. But what I could see, and see clearly, was exhaustion – and fear.

 Big, solid, dependable Tony Raglan, who'd lived on the streets of Norwich, London, and Lothing, who'd spent almost half a lifetime as a beat copper, was afraid of me.

"Tony? Look, we don't -"

"Yes. We do."

"It doesn't matter to me what you think, I'll always be there for you. No matter what."

He turned away. His voice was soft. So soft, I flinched back from the lash of it. "No, you won't."

We drove in silence. I wondered if his brain was screaming the way mine was. I'd always ducked out of relationships before things got serious enough for intense talks, but, somehow, I couldn't even think about leaving Tony.

It wasn't just that we worked together. It was who he was – he was a mystery I hadn't solved, and, good copper that I was, I wasn't prepared to walk away and leave an open case without even a handful of starting-point notes. I had a feeling solving Tony Raglan would take a lifetime, perhaps longer – most of us have ghosts that our loved ones only meet once we ourselves are shades and spirits, and I very much doubted Tony Raglan was any different.

I pulled up outside the Chinese, and spoke for the first time in about a quarter of an hour.

"Usual?"

Tony nodded, and handed me a folded twenty he took from the ashtray neither of us had any other use for. I glanced at it, stared at him.

"What's this?"

He tried for a smile, didn't quite manage to pull it off. "In case you don't like what you hear. I don't want you to feel that I owe you, if we're not together after today." He nodded towards the convenience store two doors along. "I'll get the beer."

"Tony -" but he was already walking away, and, although I knew he was close enough to hear me call after him, he didn't look back. I sighed, stuffed the twenty into my back pocket, and stepped into the takeaway.

P.C. Tony Raglan
LB 265

"I'm not going to do the whole *David Copperfield*, I was born, I grew up thing. No one's interested in that." I took a swig of my beer, and a mouthful of chicken and cashew nuts with pineapple rice. I smiled as I swallowed. "You're surprised I know that David Copperfield was a character in a Charles Dickens book, not just a stage mage, aren't you?"

Feroc shook his head. "I don't think anything about you could surprise me."

I focused on the food and the booze for the next few minutes. I didn't want to have the kind of conversation I was about to have, the kind of conversation I, we, needed to have. No one likes dragging their skeletons out of the closet to have them dance in the bright light of a lover's awareness.

Finally, I found the words I wanted, took a deep breath, and a long gulp of beer, and spoke. My voice sounded strange, as though I'd been possessed, and someone else was using my lips to speak their truth. But the truth was wholly mine: I recognised it even as I flinched from it.

"I didn't have some amazing, rural idyll childhood. We'll start with that – growing up on a farm isn't all fresh air, no rules, and getting in touch with nature." I opened another bottle of beer, shovelled more greasy food into my mouth, barely tasting either. "It's hard work, long days falling well into the night, sometimes, not much money, filth, and death. There's a hell of a lot of death, and every death has a precise loss of income attached to it. I knew by the time I'd finished primary school I wasn't going to be a farmer when I grew up." I gave a short bark of bitter laughter. "I wanted to be an actor, when I was a kid. I loved the old Western movies, and those guys seemed miles away from where I was. Where my dad was." I stared into the distance, watching nothing for a long moment, then shook my head with a rueful smile. "Anyway, that faded, the way most things of childhood do.

Someone – maybe a teacher, maybe the parent of a friend, I don't remember now – told me actors had to live in London. I'd never been farther than Norwich at this point, and the mere idea of London terrified me. Like most people in Norfolk, I imagined it as a bigger, darker version of Thetford, but with more foreigners, and guns instead of knives. I saw myself living in a basement, shivering and starving." I laughed again. "Dickens has a lot to answer for. Then, during high school, I decided I wanted to be an MP – they lived in London when they were at work, sure, but they seemed to have nice houses, be well looked after. I imagined their lives being like Sherlock Holmes', when he's played by Jeremy Brett – some woman looking after you, taking off whenever the fancy took you, lounging around reading the papers and playing the violin."

"Can you play the violin?" Feroc's hand went to his mouth, and he blushed at the interruption. I smiled, and shook my head sadly. "I can't even read music. I wanted to learn, but... well, lessons cost money, and we didn't have much. Besides, not much call for music on a farm. There's enough noise already. But, anyway, I knew MPs lived in London when they were working, but they had other houses, too. I imagined they must make a fortune – no one told us kids that the hard-working British tax payer pays for them to have their second home. And we certainly didn't know that a lot of them have a lot more than two houses. They looked smart and well-cared-for, didn't seem to have to do very much when they were at work, and they still got the whole summer off. It was like school, I reckoned, but with all the fun stuff of being an adult – having your own money, going out to restaurants and not having to sit still and shut up, alcohol, women."

"You weren't... I mean..."

"It wasn't an option. I didn't think about it the way kids seem to today – it wasn't sexual. Nothing was for us, at that age. I just imagined myself flirting with exotic, expensive women, like I'd seen in films, and one day settling down with someone kind and caring, who'd look after the kids." I snorted. "Well, as MeatLoaf told us, two outta three ain't bad." I finished my second beer, and closed my eyes. "I don't know what happened to that ambition. I lost it, somewhere. Anyway, I wasn't bright enough to go to university. So it was just as well I didn't care passionately about it, really." I turned my attention to the last of the Chinese food, fighting the urge to open a third bottle of beer. I had to work tomorrow, and turning up with a hangover would see me confined to barracks, Feroc sent out with someone else. I finished the food, got up, and paced through to the kitchen, looking for something with enough sugar to shut down the craving for poison. I heard Feroc get up and follow me. The faithful watchdog, worried for his master.

"I got a job in the pub in the village – that was the beginning of the end of what had passed for my relationship with my mother. She stopped talking to me. I'd been supposed to take over the farm, so her and dad could go and get a little bungalow somewhere. My dad hung on for a couple of years, hoping I'd come round, that I just needed to see a bit of the world before I shut myself up with the sheep and the shit... My mother attacked me the Yule of the year I'd turned eighteen. I never did go back home. I ended up in Norwich – I was still terrified of London – and, in the way of country cities in those days, the copper who found me dossing in a shop doorway decided to actually do something proactive – he took me to the hospital, got me to tell the truth about the open wound across my stomach, and gave me his address, told me to come round when the hospital let me out. I didn't want to just turn up at his house, though, in case he hadn't really meant it – so I went to the nick he'd told me he worked for, instead. And, in the way these things work out when someone else is involved -" I glanced upwards, making it clear I wasn't talking about any human agency "- it turned out to be the first decision of the rest of my life. The copper on the desk asked if I was there about the recruitment drive. I knew what the word 'recruitment' meant, and I wasn't afraid of hard work – I'd been doing it since I could walk, and for no money, at that – so I said yes." I turned and grinned. "That's how I became a copper. I went off to Hendon, and discovered London isn't as terrifying as it sounds when you grow up in a rural village where Norwich is considered a den of iniquity, with the football being the only legitimate reason for going there, did my probation at Bethel Street, in the full and certain knowledge that I was going to apply for a transfer to London. I lasted long enough to qualify as an Area car driver, and see the way the wind was blowing with Eastern European gangs and their madness moving in, and headed out here. End of part one."

I crossed the kitchen, and began to busy myself making coffee. "You want one, Feroc?"

"I want part two. I want the reasons you think I'm going to leave you. So far, I want to kill your mother, but that's about it."

"Forget about her. I'm trying to." I focused on the rhythm of stirring sugar, milk, and ground coffee beans together through hot water. Then I decided to add more sugar. Return to the rhythm, the focus. When I reached for the sugar a third time, Feroc grabbed my wrist in a grip that, although it couldn't reach all the way around, was strong enough not to need to.

"Tony – stop. Bring your coffee through, sit down, and tell me what's so bad it's making you want to kill yourself."

That shook me. Talk of suicide usually did. I picked up my mug of coffee slowly, and leaned against the counter, my eyes glazing as I started to lose myself in the mists of difficult memories.

"I did try and kill myself, for real. While I was working in London. I'd been in pursuit of a suspect – a guy who got his kicks raping women and beating them up. He'd attacked one of our WPCs." I took a deep, shaky breath, hearing the rasp of lungs against ribs, air against throat. I licked my lips, swallowed, stared into the depths of my mug as though the coffee might be home to a god, who would leap forth and save me from the words I'd have to speak tonight.

No such luck. I closed my eyes, and forced the words out. "I lost him. He just vanished. You'd have to know the streets of London, especially the East End – they're a bloody rabbit warren. I drove around for a bit, ignoring my radio, hoping I'd spot him. Nothing. I couldn't face going back, couldn't even face radioing in and admitting I'd let him get away." I bit my lip, tasting blood. "I drove the car into the river. I clocked the speed just before I went in – close to fifty. I don't know if I hit anyone – I must have done. There's no way I'd've had enough road to myself. And the car was damaged when they pulled us out." I took a gulp of coffee as though it were oxygen, as though my life depended on it. "When they came – gods alone know how they knew where to find me, maybe a member of the public had called them – I told them the bloke I'd been chasing had run me off the road. People backed coppers up, back then, unless they had a good reason not to. They found the bloke a week later – he'd gone for a fifteen year old girl. Her dad had been out walking the dog, walked right past just as it all kicked off." I swallowed, struggling to force the saliva down. "He kicked his brains out, and hanged him with the bloody dog's lead." I started laughing, hearing the edge of hysteria, but unable to stop it. "No one ever found out the truth. I applied for a transfer shortly after that."

I could hear the kitchen clock ticking. Could hear the fridge running. Could hear Feroc breathing. I felt like I was in a trance. "I made a promise to myself, the night I left London, that I would never again let a rapist get away from me. That, whatever it took, I'd be the one to wring the bastard's neck."

I turned to Feroc. "I've dealt with five rapists in the time I've been at Lothing. Four of them are dead."

"Did you -"

"Not directly, no. The thing about being a copper, if you make the right kind of effort, you'll find people who will ensure you don't have to get your own hands dirty. I know quite a lot of those people. You have to understand, Feroc, it's only recently the courts have started to get their act together when it comes to rape. It's only recently we have, if it doesn't involve one of our own. So, anyway, four of these five tykes met with some unfortunate and wholly unexpected accidents, that were nothing to do with me."

"And the fifth?"

I smiled. "Let's just say he doesn't have the required equipment to bother anyone in that way any more."

"You -"

I shook my head. "Again, not me. Working class men don't have a lot of time for people who hurt their women. And with unemployment the problem it is out here..."

Feroc was staring at me. "You broke the law."

I finished my coffee, and turned away. "The law's an ass, Feroc. Or it can be. And I didn't break a single law, not even a Code of Conduct."

"You let things happen then."

"Not on my own – I couldn't have acted alone on this, Feroc. You must know that."

"So, what other crimes merit this kind of service?"

My voice was level when I responded. "Only rape. And nonces."

"So murderers are fine, then?"

"Usually, when someone is murdered – deliberately killed – they've asked for it. There'll be something in their background that meant that they had what was coming for them."

"I'll pretend to agree with you on that, but what about people who mug old ladies?"

"They're scum, and I'm glad to see them nicked for it. So are the old dears. And they're the people that matter. They feel safe when we nick the slag. People who've been raped? They don't. They'll never feel safe again."

The hysteria was back. I clenched my hands into fists, focusing until I couldn't stand the pain of the effort any longer. I uncurled my hands. I keep my nails short, but even so, there were marks on my palms.

"Did you ever bother to ask a rape victim if they wanted vigilante action?" Feroc's voice was rough with rage. I glared into the face of his fury. "I didn't have to."

I turned away. I couldn't bear to see him walk away.

I don't know how long I stood there, facing the wall, waiting for the sound of the end of my life – but it never came. Instead, eventually, there was a soft sigh.

"I'm not going to pretend I'm happy about what you've told me. I'm not going to pretend I think it's okay, or that I think it's right.

But I know that I'm needed, if only to try and curb this vendetta of yours, help you move on from what you see as a criminal failure. Because that's where this is coming from, isn't it? You're not punishing these men, you're punishing yourself, the young copper who let a man get away who'd caused harm to a Blue. To one of the pack."

There was a sudden shock of sound as Feroc slammed his fist against the counter. "Dammit, I hate this fucking pack mentality we have going on, this idea that it's us against the world. It damages people – destroys them, even."

I whispered into the silence of the storm. "But you don't hate me?"

The pause was almost too long. "No. I don't like the way you think, right now, but I can see that my duty is to stay with you, to change the way you think."

"I'm a duty, now?"

Feroc sighed, and I thought I heard him swear under his breath. "You're a pain in the arse. I'm going to bed."

My response was immediate, and inevitable. "I'll sleep on the sofa."

Feroc walked away. He didn't even try and argue.

I opened that third beer.

P.C. Feroc Hanson
LB 599

I lay awake for a long time, feeling the emptiness of the king size bed I'd always shared with Tony. I could hear him, faintly, moving around downstairs. I heard the TV come on, then the sound cut out. He must have turned it right down. Whatever he was watching, I wouldn't share it through the murmur of white noise.

This room, our room, had always been warm. I remembered the first night we'd slept together, how Tony had opened a window the merest crack, then wrapped himself in as much of the duvet as I'd let him grab, kicking one leg and half an arm out, complaining about how hot it was. I'd stripped completely for the first time in my life, and laid beside him, a little under a third of the duvet draped over me, enjoying the feeling of residual heat. It felt like summer evenings at the beach – the sand still warm, but an edge in the cooling breeze.

Now, though, the bed, the room, were as cold as the North Sea when a storm rolls in. In the distance, faintly, I could hear the fog horn howling. Downstairs, I could hear the rise and fall of Tony's voice. I wondered who he'd called, or if he'd called anyone – perhaps he was just talking to himself. I listened harder, slowing my breathing down so I wasn't deafened by the noise blood makes as it surges through the body. No: he was too agitated to be talking to himself.

I crawled across to his side of the bed, to the faint curve his body had left in the mattress over however many years he'd had this bed. The way I'd been kicked about that first night, the bruises I'd woken with the morning after, told me Tony had long been used to sleeping alone.

I took a couple of long, deep breaths, drawing in the scent of the man I loved, but had suddenly found I didn't know.

I heard the door open just as I was falling asleep, the murmur of voices – Tony's, and a woman's. The door closed on silence.

Our bedroom was at the front of the house. I got up, and crossed over to the window. Looking out, I saw them walking off, Tony and a woman I didn't recognise. She stood side on to Tony, who had his head bowed, hands in his pockets. She had one hand half-raised, her palm towards Tony. It was a gesture Tony used, a gesture I used, a gesture coppers used, only hers was less hostile. It beckoned in, rather than holding back.

Rain fell over both of them. In the light of the street lamp, I noticed that Tony wasn't wearing a coat. His hair was already plastered to his forehead. The woman glanced up, a half smile on her lips, and pointed. Tony didn't raise his head.

Tony didn't raise his head.

That hit me like a punch to the stomach. I stepped back from the window, tears stinging the backs of my eyes, and crawled into bed, burying myself under the duvet.

When I woke the next morning, I could smell coffee, and bacon. Tony was back, then. I hadn't heard him come in. I pulled on a bathrobe – his, it turned out – and headed downstairs.

"Morning."

"Hey. You sleep okay on the sofa?"

"I didn't sleep here, in the end."

"Oh?"

"No. I thought you deserved some space, after what you heard yesterday, and I was pretty riled, to tell you the truth. I went to a friend's."

"Anyone I know?" I dropped two slices of toast into the toaster, poured a glass of milk while I waited for the electric fire to do its thing.

Tony shook his head. "No."

I badly wanted to ask him about the woman. They hadn't looked like lovers, in the light of the streetlamp, and she'd seemed to want him to know that I was watching – hardly the kind of thing you'd expect from a bit on the side. She definitely wasn't anyone from the nick, and she didn't look like a tom – she'd looked like a nice, middle-aged, middle-class woman. She'd looked a bit like my mum. Not in appearance, but in general type.

That was the hell of being gay; you lived not just in the fear that someone you loved would leave you for someone else, but that they'd turn out to be bi, and would leave you for someone you could never be.

"Does he have a name, this friend?"

Tony looked at me then. "Geraldine. And she saw you at the window, last night, so you know damn well it was a woman I went to stay with. And no, not in that way – I slept in her spare room, all very chaste and pure."

"So you called some woman I don't know, just to blag a spare room?"

"No. I called her because I needed to talk, and she's good at listening to me. We walked back to hers, we talked, she asked if I wanted to go home, I said not really, she made up the spare bed for me. I left before she woke up this morning." He turned down the heat under the bacon, picked up his mug of coffee, and turned to face me.

"Feroc, I'm *gay*, alright? I don't fancy women. And I don't cheat. Ever. I know how that feels, and I'd never do it to anyone else, alright?"

"But you still won't tell me who this Geraldine is?"

"She's a friend. I'm sure you have them, too."

I suddenly realised I didn't. I had people I'd hang around with, people I got on with, but not "friends" in the way Tony meant.

I shook my head. "You're the only person I really talk to."

Tony sighed, and took a long, slow swallow of coffee. "Well, I shouldn't be. Not for my sake, but for yours. You need someone you can slag me off to."

I watched as he finished the coffee, and began, almost immediately, making another. Tony was like that in the morning – he'd drink two mugs of coffee straight off, eat whatever he'd decided would do for breakfast that day, usually something fried or soaked in sugar, and then drink a third mug of coffee. After that, he was ready to face the day.

I, by contrast, kept my caffeine for the evenings. I never had worked out why, but it didn't stop me sleeping, so it wasn't a problem. I guessed it was something to do with the fact that I wrote best in the evening.

Do a Google image search for "writer" some time – notice how many of the pictures that feature people, writing, also feature cups of coffee. Remember TS Elliot, who apparently measured out his life in coffee spoons. Words and caffeine: they go together like a horse and carriage.

I stepped closer to Tony, breathing in the scent of grease and caffeine, and that unique smell that I would always recognise as "him", as surely as I'd recognise his voice or the sound of his footsteps. As surely as I'd always remember his call sign, even, I imagined, long after we were both retired.

With a jolt, it hit me that Tony would be in his seventies when I retired. I couldn't imagine him as an old man, his hair grey, his hearing fading, his eyes clouded by age and memories and cataracts. He was like Anne Rice's Lestat: he would always be the age he was now, immortal and eternal. And I realised that it wasn't that I refused to see him as someone who would age. It was that I refused to see him as someone who could be vulnerable.

"I don't want to slag you off. Whatever you are, whatever you do, or don't do, you have a reason for it. I just have to make the effort to find out what that reason is, and help you deal with it."

He shook his head, laughing. "It'd be easier to just slag me off. Half the time, even I don't know why I do some of the daft stuff I do. Like last night – there wasn't any need to tell you all of that. All it's done is mess with your head. You don't know if you can trust me."

"Of course I can." It was too quick, too flippant. Tony knew that. He turned away. "No, you can't. Because I can't always trust myself. And I shouldn't do – *you* shouldn't do."

I laid a hand on his shoulder, an automatic gesture of comfort. "I should trust you, though – because you could have kept that knowledge from me, but you didn't. You could have concealed that particular shadow of yourself, but you didn't. You admitted to something dark and disturbing, that you didn't have to. And that earns my trust." He glanced back at me. "So...we're okay?"

He sounded like a frightened child. I smiled. "Of course we are."
I gave his shoulder a squeeze. He smiled, and inclined his head
towards the frying pan. "You want breakfast?"

"I'll stick with toast, thanks." He shook his head. "Bread and some
kind of crap that tries to tell you it's better for you than butter.
That's not breakfast."

"I'm still stuffed from last night. I'm surprised you're not."

"So, I probably shouldn't mention that Geraldine got us both fish
and chips on the way back to hers?"

"What?!" I turned round, incredulous laughter bubbling over.
"You're kidding!"

"She'd had a busy day – hadn't had a chance to have a decent
meal. I was starting to feel peckish."

"Tony, peckish is a couple of biscuits, or some bread and cheese.
Not fish and chips, on top of a Chinese."

Tony's eyes sparkled. "See? You do need someone you can slag
me off to." He ladled bacon and eggs onto a plate, took them and
the remains of his second mug of coffee over to the poker table
that I'd sworn, the day I'd moved in properly, I was going to
replace with a proper dining table, but had never got round to. I
leant against the counter, watching him eat with a smile on my
face, and love in my heart.

Geraldine

"...so, anyway, I'm guessing you've already left for work. Give me a call when you get this, okay? I'm glad you called me last night, and I think we should try and set up something more regular. More formal. Anyway, I'll hear from you later."

I clicked to end the call, and stood, jogging the mobile in my hand, staring at its blank screen. I was worried about Tony Raglan. While he'd never let me get close, I'd picked up enough about him to know that he used food as a kind of anaesthetic when his emotions started to get the better of him. And he'd definitely been doing that last night. He'd also been pacing and biting his nails, something he'd admitted before he did when he wanted a drink, but couldn't have one for whatever reason, usually because he either was driving, or would be in a few hours. I sighed. Tony Raglan was one of the most defensive, shut-down men I'd come across, and defensive, shut-down men were pretty much my speciality. Most of them got angry as a way of expressing difficult emotions. Some of them were extremely violent when confronted by things they didn't want to accept or deal with.

Tony Raglan wasn't violent. He didn't get angry in the way many of the men I worked with did, the raging, screaming maelstrom of wild energy. His anger was cold. Ice cold. And far more terrifying than the white heat that could see fists and tables flying at a moment's notice.

I wondered, not for the first time, if Tony Raglan self-harmed – other than the unhealthy eating habits. He certainly had plenty of what I termed "normalised risk behaviours": he liked driving faster than was sensible, he gambled, he would spend money regardless of whether he could afford it. There was the poor diet, of course, the over-reliance on junk food. He played rugby, a contact sport. There were probably other things I didn't know about, things he'd never willingly tell anyone, much less me.

I'd come up with the concept of normalised risk behaviours for what we more typically think of as self-harm five years into my practice, about fifteen years ago, and they'd rapidly gained favour in psychiatric circles. Other psychiatrists started examining their own patients, and seeing a marked correlation between normalised risk behaviours and actual self-harming.

I called them normalised risk behaviours because they were socially-acceptable ways of putting the physical body in the way of danger: they were a way of experiencing the *feelings* associated with cutting or burning or purging, without having to navigate the often tricky logistics of those behaviours.

When your mate or your subordinate keeps nipping to the loo, and is always wearing long sleeved shirts, even in the height of summer, you start to worry. When they put their foot down behind the wheel, or shove another chocolate bar in their mouth, not so much. You might tease them, but you don't worry about them.

Tony Raglan ran up a lot of red flags, despite the fact that, for the most part, he was very good at talking a lot without saying very much. I needed to get him to open up, to trust me. I needed to know he would ask for my help if the things he couldn't face were driving him to do things that were actually and actively putting him in harm's way.

Most of all, though, I needed him to start being honest with the young man he'd talked about last night, presumably the same young man I'd seen at the upstairs window. Feroc. Feroc Hanson, who'd been with him during the accident last year, and who had pledged a deeper allegiance to him in the aftermath of the shooting that had followed.

I hoped they survived as a couple, whilst knowing it wouldn't be easy for either of them. Tony saw that. Feroc possibly didn't. He was young, perhaps yet young enough to believe that being gay didn't matter.

I hoped time wouldn't prove him too badly wrong.

P.C. Feroc Hanson
LB 599

We'd been out on patrol for a couple of hours. Everything was fairly quiet, and so Tony had pulled up on the seafront, and we sat in the Area car, watching the waves rise and fall. Tony was taking swigs from a can of Coke. I was just enjoying the sights, sounds and scents of what was still a traditional British seafront.

"You alright, Tony?"

He sighed., and finished the Coke. "Can you imagine if they really did put cocaine in this stuff?"

"Tony?"

"I mean, personally, I reckon we should legalise drugs. People are more likely to take them *because* they're illegal. It's like JagerMeister."

"That's not illegal."

"It should be – people go more mental on that stuff than they ever do on half the drugs that *are* banned. Anyway, my point is, Jager tastes like someone threw up and then had their cat piss in it. No one in their right mind would drink it. Apart from the fact that there's this mystique been created around it, that you're well 'ard if you can do a shot of Jager. You're up for a bit of rabble rousing. So, people drink JagerMeister, even though it makes you feel even worse than it tastes."

"This from the guy who drinks Bombay Sapphire and pineapple juice."

"Only if I'm not drinking lager. And anyway, I'm not the only one."

"Oh, I have a feeling you probably are."

"And I know I'm not. Max got me into that drink – it was his first. Anyway, as I was saying, people drink Jager because there's this cult around it. They do drugs for the same reason. If they legalised drugs – boom, the cult's disbanded, and the only people buying drugs are people who know what they're doing. And they know they're getting something safe. And you've got a way of keeping tabs on who's taken what, and how much, if you find them blacked out on the street somewhere. No one has to mug old ladies to buy their next fix, because legalising something makes it more affordable. I mean, c'mon, half the prescription drugs we have these days have an opium base. Opium is heroin by any other name."

"I don't think it's a good idea. I mean, drugs kill people.

"So do cars. We're not banning those, are we?"

It clicked, then. "Is that what this is about? That POL-AC?"

Tony didn't answer for a while. When he did, it was the briefest nod. No words.

"No one's ever died before, Feroc. I've had prangs, sure, but I've never killed someone. Two people, technically."

"Steven Lassiter killed himself, Tony."

"Yeah, but he wouldn't have done if that girl hadn't died."

"You don't know that."

"He's been inside before. He'd've come out and got on with his life."

"Maybe, maybe not."

"I lost it, Feroc. Lost control. And I've never lost it that badly before. So badly that someone died."

"You couldn't've avoided what happened, Tony."

"Yes, I could! I could've held back! I could've abandoned pursuit – I probably should've abandoned pursuit! But I didn't!"

"No, because that's not the kind of copper you are. It's not the kind of driver you are, and it's why you're such a damn good driver. It's why everyone, even from other divisions, wants to have you behind the wheel on their jobs. Even CID, and that's saying something." I laid a hand on Tony's shoulder. "Look, Tony, you're a brilliant driver. Everyone knows that. You're a legend. And the thing is, you don't get to be a legend, in any sphere, without being willing to take risks. You take risks, and sometimes those risks pay off, and elevate you to brilliance. But you never even get close to that if you refuse to take risks. You have to play a few wild cards to make a rep. And you've got one hell of a rep."

"Do you believe that? That -" Tony took a deep breath, shaking as he exhaled "- that I'm good at what I do?"

I stared at him in stunned surprise. "Of course I do! The whole nick does. How could you ever doubt that?"

He sighed, and looked away. "Sometimes, it just feels like I'm making it up as I go along, drifting from one screw up to another. It doesn't *feel* like I'm good at what I do. It feels like I'm firing a semi-automatic at a barn door: enough shots, enough space – I'm bound to hit it at least a few times. I have moments of brilliance in a sea of screw ups."

"No!" He jumped at my shout. I never shouted. "No." My voice was quieter that time, but the edge was still there. "That's not true. Don't ever let them make you believe that – the Beresfords of this world, the brass, the tabloid scum, the slag out there. The voices in your head. Tell them all to shut up and sit down, because you're the best damn beast in the room, and you're going to prove it, over and over and over again."

Tony gave a shaky laugh. "Wow. You're really passionate about this, aren't you?"

"I'm passionate about you."

"Lima-Bravo One from Lima-Bravo, you're in the vicinity of the Marina, aren't you? Report of a break in on board a cruiser moored there, berth 4C – that's four-charlie. The boat's called the *Kahlo Dali.* Informant the harbour master, a Mr. James O'Neal."

I saw Tony's eyes flash. "That's Max's boat." I snatched up the radio. "Lima-Bravo from Lima-Bravo received. We're right next door to the Marina, over. ETA one minute. Over."

"Received, Lima-Bravo One."

We didn't bother with the car.

P.C. Tony Raglan
LB 265

I hoped Max had headed off to Norwich for the day. I wondered what he had on board the *Kahlo Dali* that was worth nicking.

I'd never been able to pin down exactly what I was feeling where Max was concerned, and I couldn't now. That had been part of the reason for our split – not the only reason, not by a long shot, but one of them. Part of the whole mess of stuff that human beings call "a reason", because there's a hundred different things going on, and you can't begin to untangle any one of them from all the others.

I wasn't in love with Max any longer, and the way things were playing out with Feroc, I don't think I ever had been – I'd been fascinated by him, in the original sense of the word. He had a charm that was all his own, and it was easy to get lost in him, and his reality. But no. I wasn't in love with him. All the same, I still liked the bloke, and I didn't want harm to come to him. I didn't want him to end up as collateral damage in someone else's war.

That had been another reason in "the reason": the increasing likelihood of Max ending up as collateral damage.

As we jogged along the gangway that granted foot access to the berths, I glanced up at Waveney Court. The windows with the stylised sunrise decals of Eastern Rise Investments had their blinds pulled. No glint of light showed beyond the beige fabric. That struck me as odd: people tended to get awfully worried about their money when they'd entrusted it to someone else. Taking a weekday off seemed a bit...strange. But, then, what did I know about finance? Maybe the office was only there for meetings – you could probably run a business like that with a smartphone, a bank account, and a bit of nous.

I saw Max before we actually reached the *Kahlo Dali*; he was sitting on a camping chair at the back of the boat, his head in his hands, a radio playing classical music. Too sombre for Classic FM: must be Radio 4. Feroc listened to the same two stations. It surprised me how traditional arty types could be. Personally, I was a rock man. The proper stuff – Guns 'n' Roses, Judas Priest, Black Sabbath, a bit of MeatLoaf, some Lemmy. All the old, bad boys who actually had something to say.

"Max! What's going on?" I made the short jump from the gangway to the deck in one fluid motion – though not quite as fluid as Feroc: the cocky git didn't even break stride. I raised an eyebrow. "What, were you a long jump champion before you joined up?" I turned back to Max. "What's happened?"

He lifted his head – for the first time in the years I'd known him, he looked tired. "I'd been in the city – London, not Norwich – for a few days. I came back, and the door was busted open. Doesn't look like they took anything, though. Dunno why the harbour master called you lot – I only reported it in case whoever it was tried another boat, where there was actually something to nick. And so that he'd get the marina owners to fork out for a new door."

I stepped closer, and noticed that Max was holding himself awkwardly. He winced every time he breathed.

"Max, has someone given you a going over?"

"No." It was too quick. "I fell down the stairs at the youth hostel I was staying in. In London. I was drunk – stupid kind of accident I should've grown out of by now."

"And the hostel can confirm that? It'll be in their accident log?"

"Nah – like I said, I was drunk. I felt enough of a prat without going and telling anyone about it."

"So you didn't report it?"

"No. Like I said, no harm, no foul. I wasn't in too much pain, there was no blood, so I just picked myself up and got on with my life."

"But you're in pain now?"

"Just a bit stiff and sore. The bruising coming out, I expect. Nothing I can't handle."

I clocked the bottle of Bombay Sapphire and carton of pineapple juice, along with the skull-shaped glass I'd bought for Max the first Valentine's Day we had together, that were clustered on a low table beside his easel.

"Go easy on that stuff, yeah? If you're in pain, see a doctor."
Max grunted out a laugh. "With the waiting times round here?
Sitting in a room full of chavs snotting on the floor, their brats
running around everywhere, then having some patronising GP
clock the "Homosexually identified" note on my record, and
waste six of my ten minutes asking about am I practising safe sex,
and when was the last time I had a HIV test?" He shook his head.
"Nah, I don't think so."

Something about Bombay Sapphire and skulls was ringing bells...
"When did you get back from London?"

"This morning. 10.45am. No, I don't still have my tickets – I'm not
an anally-retentive paranoid like you. I don't keep things that
would prove where I've been and what I've been doing. I have this
old-fashioned notion that people might just believe me."

Yeah. That was another reason in the mess I called "the reason."
What do they call it in divorce proceedings? 'Irreconcilable
differences.'? That pretty much summed up Max and me.

"And you left when?"

"Friday, Saturday. One of those days. It was packed – the train, I
mean."

"Which hostel did you stay at?"

"I dunno. It was in King's Cross. None of the ones near Liverpool
Street had beds. It was near a kebab shop."

"So you definitely weren't in Lothing yesterday?"

"No, I was in London yesterday. I'm hardly ever in Lothing, these
days. I've got a flat in Norwich. And a studio. I keep the boat here
because I prefer the view, and it's quicker to get out to sea if I
need to take off for a day or so. What *is* all this about me being in
Lothing?"

"Nothing."

"You're a crap liar, Tony. You always were."

"Yeah, and you were too damn good."

We stared at each other for a while, lost in angry memories and
disappointed hopes. Finally, Feroc broke the spell with a cough.

I nodded to him, took a breath, and pulled myself together. "Mind if we look around?"

"Be my guest. You remember where everything is? I don't have the same opportunities to move stuff about on a boat. It's all pretty much where it was the last time you were here."

I followed Max down into the main living space, ducking my head to clear the narrow doorway, already feeling claustrophobic. Feroc followed me, looking around with sharp, bright eyes. He'd clearly never been on a boat before, or at least not one someone spent more than a few hours at a time on.

"What're you working on at the moment?"

"Commissions. Close copies of old masters."

"Forgeries."

"No. Close copies. The client knows they're not the real deal, I don't charge him as if they are, and I include small details that would make it obvious to anyone with half a brain that the painting couldn't've been done by Picasso, Cezanne, Matisse, Rothko, Dali. Anachronisms, contemporary references, that sort of thing."

"Sounds like forgery to me. Just clever enough to be legal."

Behind me, Feroc spoke. "It's what artists do, Tony. Hardly anyone makes money from creative stuff if they just focus on what they want to do. I mean, when I thought I was going to be a professional writer, I'd write students' essays for them, reviews of places I'd never been, things I'd never used, shows I'd never seen... it's bread and butter stuff, but it pays the bills."

Max looked past me to Feroc. "You're a writer?"

"I'm a copper. Sometimes I write."

"Why'd you decide not to do it professionally?"

Feroc laughed. "I don't cope well with crowded, highly-competitive marketplaces."

"But you do still write? Sometimes?"

"Yeah. I actually have a book out – POD deal, but it's sold a few copies."

"What's it called? I might get you another sale."

"*New Blues* – it's basically a slightly sexed-up version of the diary I kept during my probation."

I shook my head. "God help us all."

"You, especially – I wish I'd known how things were going to play out with us while I was writing that."

Max was grinning. "Stop it, you," I snarled, without any real menace. He laughed.

"You want to get a hobby, Tony. Feroc'll tell you, having something to do to switch off is a balm to the soul."

"I've got plenty of hobbies."

Max raised a hand, counting on fingers. "Driving. Watching other people drive better cars than you can afford. Reading about cars. That's not a hobby, Tony – that's work."

"Yeah? Well, right now, my work is finding out what happened here. So: have you been telling me the truth, the whole truth, and nothing but the truth, as heard by your gods and mine?"

"I was in London. I was there over the weekend, I got back this morning. I fell down the stairs at a youth hostel I was staying in."

I noted that he didn't simply say "Yes." That was telling. Telling enough? I wasn't certain on that one, not yet.

"How often do you get back to the boat? Since you sound like you're pretty well set up in Norwich, these days?"

"There are such things as trains, Tony. And the A12."

"A47."

"What?"

"It's the A47 now. They renamed it, at least the part of it that runs through here. Trying to appeal to the tourists by making it sound as though we're all metropolitan and well-connected."

"Can they even spell 'metropolitan' round here?"

"Not likely. Most of them can barely write their name in the sand with a stick."

"What do they want tourism for, anyway? I thought they had enough problems with traffic – they whine about it enough, at any rate."

"They keep threatening to develop the Point, If they get more tourists, they might have the money to carry the threats through."

Max passed a hand over his eyes. "Oh, worlds above and below – why? Why do they *always* want to tear the heart out of something that's naturally beautiful and perfect just as it is? For a bunch of silly twats with cameras and ADHD."

"I know. I hear you."

"But no one hears us, do they? No one hears the people who value the Point just as it is. No one hears the bird watchers, the photographers, the people who just want to step off the merry-go-round for a few minutes. No one's interested, because we're not handing over bloody money all the while."

"I take it you still paint there, then?"

"During storms, yes. The sea there's beautiful with a strop on."

"They might recreate the old fishing village."

Max snorted. "They won't. People round here think the only history that matters was the last time England won the World Cup. Anything beyond that's boring, as far as they're concerned."

We stood in silence for a while, the three of us, Feroc taking in the boat, the details of Max's life – probably storing them away to use in his writing. I was taking in Max. Max – well, I wasn't sure about Max. He could've been lost in thought, he could've simply been taking in the sound of the waves just beyond the marina, the motion of the boat, the screams of the seagulls overhead.

"Why would someone rob the *Kahlo Dali*, Tony? I mean, there's a score of boats that're obviously owned by people far better off than me. They're more likely to have stuff worth nicking."

"Crimes like this, where nothing's taken, usually happen because the perpetrator knows the victim, and wants to send a message. Are you in trouble, Max?"

"No."

"By Thor's name?"

"I told you, Tony, no!"

Again, an interesting refusal to commit to his answer. Just the anger of a child who can't accept that their lie isn't good enough. But that, in itself, was odd: Max had never lied badly. He either told the truth, or a lie so well-crafted it passed for the truth for a bloody long time. This? This actually *was* childish, in the truest sense of the word: it was a child, lying.

"Well, we'll give the harbour master a crime number – the

insurers'll want that. If you need cash to sort the door before then, give me a shout, yeah?"

"I'm not a charity case, Tony."

I sighed. "No, but you are someone I care for. Someone who was under my protection once, and remains within my concern. So, if I can help you in this fashion, I will do so. You know it to be within my power, and no hardship to me."

"I hate it when you get all formal."

You used to love it, I thought. *It used to be our language. Our world.*

"We'll be off, if there's nothing you want to add?"

"What would I add? I've told you what happened."

"Sure."

As we stepped off the gangway and headed back to where we'd left the car, Feroc turned to me. "Operating with fifty percent info. Nice."

"I doubt it's as high as that. But it's what we've got."

"What do you think happened? On the level?"

"On the level? I think Max pissed off the wrong people, and they gave him a hiding. We'll probably never find out who those people are, or what the hiding was about."

"You think he did the burglary?"

I paused. "I don't think so. He didn't seem worried when we asked if he'd been in Lothing. I think he *was* here, but not robbing Angela Dalloway."

"The gin, though -"

"They sell it in Tesco's in the high street. We've got a bottle at home. Probably hundreds of other people have."

"But he does like skulls. That glass -"

"I brought that for him. He was going through a Goth phase when we first got together."

"He still has it, though."

"A lot of people like skulls. It doesn't mean they nick them. Max probably doesn't even know Angela Dalloway – Beresford Avenue's not the kind of place you take a casual Sunday stroll, is it? And if he did know her, and wanted that skull? He'd charm it from her. Men like Max don't need to steal."

All the same, as we got into the car, I couldn't help thinking about those tarot decks. Why would someone who wasn't in to that sort of thing – and most criminals aren't – bother picking them up? If you thought they were valuable, you'd just shove them in a bag and be on your way.

I felt anxious, and decided to see if anything had come back on the blood or fingerprints found at the scene yet. The blood might not mean anything: Max's type was fairly common – the same as Feroc's, as it went. And I knew Max didn't have a criminal record, so we'd have to have reasonable grounds to pull him in and get a DNA sample to try and match to. A liking for skulls and gin, even though those things were stolen, wasn't reasonable grounds, not in anyone's book. Even an A-Level Law student would hang us out to dry if we gave Max a tug with just that to go on.

"Lima-Bravo One from Lima-Bravo, receiving? Report of a disturbance at the Santander branch in the high street, over."

"Received, Lima-Bravo. Show us dealing."

Max

I watched the Area car drive past from the deck of the *Kahlo Dali;* they were heading back into town.

 I was shaking. I knew Tony hadn't been fooled – my lies had sounded obvious even to me. You'd have to be a complete idiot to be taken in by them, and Tony Raglan was far from an idiot.

 I took a deep, shaky breath. I shouldn't have done it... It'd just seemed like my only option, at the time. If only I hadn't met Garret. I'd've never've been round his place, would never have been in that shop, would never've heard that silly cow wittering on about her money in the biscuit tin, how she was going to book herself one of them coach holidays, next year, if things worked out between now and then.

 I paced around to the stern, where my easel and radio – and my poisoned chalice – were set up, and slumped back into the chair I'd been sitting in when Tony and his boy had first turned up. I'd order the lad's book – it might well make for interesting reading, and I was keen to see if he had any kind of real talent. I suspected he did – he had that quiet confidence, the kind that didn't need to shout about itself. It was probably what had drawn Tony to him – he'd admitted it was part of what had drawn him to me.

 With a groan, I ran my hands through my hair – and yelped as the motion of raising my arms to head height tugged on what I was beginning to strongly suspect was a broken rib or three.

 I should get to a hospital, get myself checked out. But I'd have to explain how I'd come by the injuries, and I doubted a doctor would believe I'd fallen down some stairs. Tony wouldn't, if he got a chance to see me without a shirt on: boot prints tend to be quite unmistakable, especially when they're kicked into human flesh.

 They certainly look absolutely nothing like stairs of any kind.
I sighed, and pulled my phone out of my pocket. Later, I'd order Feroc Hanson's book.

 Now, though, I had to try and get myself out of this mess I'd somehow landed in. Without the help of the one man I trusted.

P.C. Feroc Hanson
LB 599

I waited until we were well clear of the Marina before I spoke.
"Tony -"
"Don't."
"Tone -"
"Look, I know he's lying. I know there's more going on than he's telling us now, or is ever going to tell us. I know he didn't get his injuries falling down a set of stairs in London. I know he probably wasn't even *in* London. But we'll never get him to admit to any of that, so, for now, we just have to take it at face value."
"But -"
"But nothing. None of it really matters, at the end of the day. We'll pass the details on to CID, they'll decide what to do next. Out of our hands. Definitely out of mine – conflict of interest, all that old malarkey."
"He's an ex."
"And probably a con. Probably always has been. The Force has only just begun to settle down and calm its collective nerves about the idea of gay coppers. Gay coppers involved in an investigation into their bent ex? The press'd have a field day."
"You reckon he wasn't on the level even when you were together?"
"I doubt very much that Max Rockford has been on the level since he became a legal adult."
"But you didn't do anything about it? You didn't call him on it?"
Tony shook his head. "No. I turned a blind eye, made excuses. All the things we tell people – mostly women – not to do. But I thought I loved him."
"Thought?"
"Yeah."
"You mean you didn't?"
"No. Not really. I loved being part of his scene. I loved the lifestyle I got to enjoy being 'Max Rockford's boyfriend.' It was so radically different from anything I'd ever know – I suppose I was

kind of drunk on it. That was what I was in love with, if I was in love with anything. Not Max. Not really. But that life..." Tony shook his head again, the meaning different this time. "That life was a beautiful disaster."

I understood something about the man I worked and lived with, the man I wanted to marry, the man I would give my life for.

"You get off on danger, on the thrill of maybe being caught."

Tony glanced at me. "Yes."

When we pulled into the high street, the crowd outside the bank told us that things hadn't resolved themselves while we were en route. We got out of the car, Tony making sure to lock it behind us, and pulled on our caps as we walked forward, that slow, deliberate swagger that almost all cops copy off John Wayne. Because this is our town, our manor. And it ain't big enough for us and trouble.

We were greeted by a weasel in a suit – the manager, I guessed. He seemed reluctant to be soothed by Tony's corporation-issue, soothe-the-customers smile.

"What seems to be the problem?" I practised Tony's tone of voice with that phrase in the shower. The casual, friendly implication that, probably, most likely, there isn't actually a problem at all, but the big boys are here to have a look anyway, make sure everything's alright. Don't worry, no one's cross. I was close to his level of lilt, but not spot on. Not yet.

"There's a...well...a...person...making rather a fuss. You see, my staff aren't certain that they are the individual named on their bank card, you see, and -"

"Laura? Laura Raith?"

A woman with a pony tail that looked like it had been forged in the halls of the Valkyries on a bad day, turned from her argument with a blocky security guard who seemed to be doing a fancy dress impersonation of a gorilla, without the fancy dress. I took in several things about her at once: one, she was easily as tall as Tony. Two, her hands, which were half-curled into fists at her sides, looked awkwardly large against the cuffs of her fitted, long-sleeve, tattoo-design t-shirt. Three, several other customers were smirking, and had their smartphones out.

"Oi – you lot: let's put the phones away, yeah? Nothing to see here. Unless you want to get an eyeful of the inside of a police station for invasion of privacy?"

"It's in a public place, innit? Shouldn't come out if it don't wanna be filmed."

The woman spun on one square, low heel. "Yeah? Maybe you don't want to come out if you don't want to end up with your teeth half way down your throat."

"Come on then, mate, if you think you've got the balls."

There was a round of sniggering. "Right – you lot – OUT."

"We got legitimate business here, copper."

Tony stepped over, fury in his eyes. "You couldn't even spell 'legitimate business', pal. Out. Now. Or I nick the lot of you – with extreme prejudice. Your choice."

Tony was bigger than the mouthy guy, who suddenly revised his belief that bravado was a good idea. "Fuck this. Some fucking faggot he-she – it ain't worth it."

He sauntered out, a couple of other customers following him.

"Oh, fantastic – now I'm losing business, too!"

Tony turned and glared at the manager. "You're not a pub. I don't think it's going to hurt your bonus. And in case it's escaped your notice, this lady is a customer, too."

The gorilla smirked – then he saw Tony's expression, and decided that he had some urgent business in a back room somewhere.

Tony crossed over to the woman. "You alright?"

"Oh yeah. Wonderful. Some bitch on the counter decides to kick off that I "don't look like the individual they have listed as the card holder for my account", and I get to be the bad guy. Just the kind of day I want when I'm trying to pay in a cheque, like any normal human being."

"You had another form of ID with you, yeah? Passport, driving licence?"

"Both. You realise trannies and terrorists are the only people who are expected to always have photographic proof of ID on them, literally all the time? And we both get the law called on us because someone doesn't like our face."

Tony walked over to the counter. "So, let me get this right: a customer comes in to your bank, and asks to pay a cheque into an account. The name on the cheque, and the name on the account, are exactly the same. It's highly unlikely that any kind of fraud or crime is being committed, but you decide to scream for your boss, who, in turn, decides to bother us. Why was that, exactly?"

"Well, the account holder is identified as a female customer, and..."

"And you, and your boss, have very set ideas about what women can look like? With attitudes like that, I'm amazed we don't get called here more often, the state of some of the women round here. My next door neighbour and her daughter clearly bank elsewhere – they look a lot like Ms. Raith, only not as tall. And without Ms. Raith's ability to pull an outfit together."

I had to agree, the woman did look stylish, even in clearly casual clothes. The dark blue denim of her jeans set off the base grey of her top, and her boots were smartly stylish. Her handbag was small and unremarkable, a neat, square leather job in muted primary colours. Even her make up was subtle yet striking – eyes outlined simply in kohl, a hint of pale lipstick. She wore pearl studs.

Her hands didn't match, that was all. Her hands, and her voice. And her height – there really weren't many women of six-four who'd opt to wear even low heels.

"I know Ms. Raith. I've known her for over fifteen years. Now, I can offer my own ID as a guarantor that she's not attempting to impersonate anyone, or commit any crime." Tony was holding his warrant card with an air of casual threat. "I suggest you let her go about her lawful business, pay her cheque in, and be on her way."

He turned to the woman. "Do you want to make a complaint?" She shook her head, and approached the counter again. "No. If I howled to the police every time someone decided to be an arsehole, I'd never get anything else done."

Weasel-in-a-suit tutted. I wheeled on him. "You, shut it."

"I must protest -"

"And I must remind you to shut up, unless you want to see police brutality in action."

Tony turned to me, an expression of surprised approval on his face. The woman – Laura – was smirking, too.

"You get more like me every day, Feroc. The brass are going to want to do something about that, sooner or later."

We stayed until Laura had concluded her transaction. Tony walked with her to the door, I followed a short way behind.

"Do you want us to give you a lift home?"

"No. I'm usually fine if I keep walking. At least dressed like this, anyway."

"Was anything ever done about that?"

"No."

"Do you want me to have a word?"

"Thanks, but it's not worth the hassle. I won't go to Southtown. And, if I do, I won't wear nice clothes. The guy was drunk, I was stupid to have gone somewhere like that in a dress -"

"You've got the right to wear whatever you want. Same as anyone else."

"No, I haven't. Nor have the women who get raped when they're wearing miniskirts and crop tops. It's funny, isn't it? I'm 'not a real woman', but I'm expected to curtail my self-expression, just the same as any other woman is."

I drew level with Tony, and watched the woman walk out. She held her head high, and her stride was certain. Tony turned back to the manager.

"Next time, show some basic courtesy, and leave your prejudices at the door when you come to work. And have your staff do the same. I'm not going to be happy if I'm called out for something like this again, okay?"

"Y-yes."

"And don't even think about making a complaint, because I can lay so many charges against you, you won't even know what day it it is. C'mon, Feroc – let's get out of here."

Once we were back in the car, I turned to Tony.

"That woman..."

"Laura. Laura Raith."

"She..." I searched for the right words. "She hasn't always been a woman, has she?"

"No. No more than anyone has 'always been' the way they are now. 'Now', as I'm sure a bright lad like you must realise, is a very finite space of time. We grow into our now-ness, and we grow out of it, too."

"Was she called Laura when you met her?"

"Not relevant."

"How did you meet her? Them?"

"Her. In a gay bar, as it goes."

"I can't see you going to gay bars, somehow."

"Who said either of us was there for pleasure? She was working, so was I."

"When you say 'working'..."

"I mean, mopping up beer and vomit. You're as bad as that lot back there." Tony was angry – beyond angry. There was a wild edge to his voice that sent chills through me.

"That's not fair – I don't have a problem with people like Laura."

"Don't you?"

"No!"

"So, you regularly assume that any woman working in a bar is on the game?"

"No, but -"

"Then you have a problem with women like Laura. And you need to take a good, long look at why that is."

I tried to change tack. "So, did you and Laura -?"

"No, we didn't date. Laura's straight. As in, she pursues sexual and romantic relationships with straight men. I, as you may have noticed, am gay. That, in case you're unsure, means I don't date women. It doesn't matter to me whether they have the requisite parts, or simply identify and present as women – I don't want to be with someone who presents and identifies as a woman. Ever. That's why I'm gay, as opposed to bi."

I grinned. "Or pan."

"What?"

"Pansexual. That's a thing, now."

Tony sighed. "Is it actually a thing in the real world, or just on social media? There is a difference. And what does it mean, anyway? Attracted to kitchen utensils?"

"No. It's being attracted to everyone – men, women, trans people, non-binary people, gender non-conforming people – the whole deal."

"Right. Yeah, well, I'm not that, either."

"So, you met Laura in a bar when you were both working – how'd you go on to actually know each other?"

"We got talking. We had stuff in common – she happens to like classic motors. We met up at a few shows over the years, had a few beers together. How do most people get to know each other?"

I stared out of the window for a long while. Finally, I said; "I've never met a trans person before."

Tony swung the Area car into the rear yard of the nick. "You probably have – you just didn't realise it."

We got out of the car, Tony stretching and yawning. "Anyway, all you need to know is that you're expected to be polite, and play nicely. They're probably not remotely interested in a skinny runt like you, and, if they are, you're already in a relationship, so you can politely but firmly refuse. Now, let's get some grub – I'm starving."

D.C. Tam Freud

I glanced through the narrow window in the door to reception before I opened it, a long-time habit of wanting to see exactly what kind of creature I was dealing with, and assess whether it was likely to want to maul me or seduce me.

Alexander Clifford-Alistair looked exactly like every other smug idiot who thinks that being paid well, and getting to wear a suit every day, makes them some kind of epitome of successful, and worthy of respect.

Sorry, Mr. Clifford-don't-you-know-it's-hypenated-Alistair, you're about to find out that I'm the kind of chick who can have more respect for someone starving in the gutter than any number of people cruising the top strata of the property market and dodging tax. I'd had the kind of childhood that teaches you, from an early age, that there's low life in high places. And that lesson had been consistently reinforced as I'd become a teenager, a young adult, and, finally, a functional, adult woman, with a job, a mortgage, and a habit of losing pens and keys.

Clifford-Alistair sat with his legs spread, lounging back against the cheap plastic seat, arms folded across a paunch he had no intention of admitting to. His blond hair was artfully styled, probably to conceal the fact that he was going bald. His suit was off the rack, but his shirt and shoes had that if-you-have-to-ask-the-price-you-can't-afford-it gleam. The blending made my ears prick up. Sure, maybe our boy Alex didn't bother to splash out on pure workwear, preferring to spend his cash on clothes that might get an airing in casual settings, too. But I felt it was much more likely the mixture of affordability and high style spoke of someone not really used to money, who had recently started to acquire a significant amount of it. And yes, there were any number of explanations for that, too, and it was only my life experience and inherent prejudice that led me down the dark alleys of the more nefarious ones.

I opened the door, and breezed through.

"Mr. Clifford-Alistair?"

He looked up, frowning. "Yes?"

I held out a hand, all bright-smiles and value judgements. "D.C. Tam Freud. I was told you wanted to speak to CID about an incident outside your place of work ycsterday?"

"My place of *business*, officer. I do not 'work' – I do business. For myself, and for my clients." He paused. "Look, I... Well, I'm sure you're very good at your day to day bits and pieces, but, the thing is, this does involve quite high-level finance, so -"

"So my double major from Oxford in Pure Mathematics and Applied Mathematics, and the five years I spent working in one of the pre-eminent trading houses of the London Stock Exchange, wouldn't really be relevant?"

He started, stared, and began to stutter. "I – I'm sorry, I -"

Syrup smiles from yours truly. "I understand, sir. Quite a few people are surprised to find that some police officers already do have degrees – the papers make it sound like we're a bunch of head-banging thickos, don't they?" I had long experience in *not* saying "That's okay, sir – most people don't realise that it is possible to be physically attractive and intelligent at the same time. Especially when those people have XY chromosomes." That never really went down too well.

 "I didn't mean any offence, you understand -"

"Of course not, sir." I held the door open. "If you'd like to follow me?"

Max

I could see from the boat that Al wasn't in his office. I tried his number, but his phone just rang through. Must be on silent – that meant he was with a client, and, if he wasn't seeing them at the office, that meant he could be anywhere.

I slammed my hand against the deck rail in frustration. With a sudden resolve, I ducked below deck, through the strip of plywood that would serve as a door until someone got round to coming out to replace the one that had been kicked in, and snatched up my jacket, which had once been Tony Raglan's. It was at least two sizes too big, but I like the way the leather was worn in, fading in patches. And it had been at least half a size too small for him when I took it.

I shot the cheap bolt on the plywood, and bounded across the deck and onto the gangway.

"Mr. Rockford! The carpenters will be out tomorrow to see to your door. The Marina are fine about paying for the damage."

I paused. "Good. That's what I pay my fees for." I carried on, moving at a fast lope. If Al was in Lothing, I'd find him, even if it took me all day. There weren't too many places that a financial advisor would meet with a client in Lothing.

Of course, if he wasn't meeting with a legitimate client, that widened the scope of places he could be. I paused after I stepped off the gangway, considering which way to head.

I turned towards Kellen Run. There was a cafe and art gallery that I knew Al frequented. I'd been there with him a couple of times.

I slowed my pace, a quiet feeling of determination coming over me. Even if Al wasn't there, I had a feeling someone there would be able to tell me where he was. Or where he might be.

The Banana Lounge was a short walk from the beach, in a part of the run down area of Kellen Run that was currently emerging from the painful chrysalis of shifting its identity from "avoid if you value your life" to "up and coming creative centre." I noted that the owners of The Banana Lounge had added a small deli since I'd last been there.

"What can I get you?" I cast my gaze around the room, but the only people in at this time of day were a couple of old dears and a young Goth girl who was sitting alone, legs stretched out, stirring a mug of hot chocolate with grim determination.

"Ah, can I get a white hot chocolate, and a pepperoni pizza roll?" Pepperoni pizza rolls were a Banana Lounge special – basically, it was a slice of pepperoni pizza, wrapped in light, flaky pastry, which was then drizzled with melted cheese. They were rich, sinful, and utterly delicious. I smiled, remembering that Tony had never ordered fewer than three of them at a time.

"Is that to eat in, or take away?"

"Ah, I'll grab a seat here, if that's okay?"

"Of course – we don't just keep the chairs and tables for decoration." I laughed along with Richard, the owner of The Banana Lounge, and pulled out a chair. "You haven't seen the bloke from Eastern Rise Investments in here recently, have you? He wasn't at his office, and I need to talk to him."

"Remind me?"

"Blond, going to seed, expensive shoes."

"Ah, Mr. Hyphenated. No, I've not seen him for a couple of weeks. Sorry."

I forced a smile."No worries – I'll leave a message at the office. I'm sure he'll get back to me. Cheers." I inhaled the mingling scents of sweet hot chocolate and savoury pepperoni as Richard brought both to my table. I felt restless, anxious. I wanted to head off and look for Al, but I knew I'd hunt better once I'd had something to eat and drink. All the same, I didn't plan to linger.

"It's Max, isn't it? You did an exhibition with us back in the summer."

"Yeah – I'm surprised you remember."

"Why wouldn't I? You sold pretty well. Good work, too. You going to exhibit again? Got Christmas coming up."

"Yule. Yeah..." I sighed, then smiled. "I could probably have something rustled up. Can I provisionally book the first two weeks in December?"

Richard pulled out a large leather diary, and flipped through, pencil at the ready. "No problem. It's one-fifty for two weeks, but you can pay nearer the time."

"Thanks." I flipped open my wallet, and pulled out three twenties. "I'll pay fifty upfront. And the other ten's for the hot chocolate and the roll. Keep the change."

"I was sorry to hear about Tony Raglan getting shot – shocking, that was. You don't expect that sort of thing in a place like this. Not guns. He used to come in here with you, didn't he? When we first opened."

"A lifetime ago. We're... we haven't been together for a couple of years, now."

"He bought one of your paintings in the summer."

I looked up in surprise. "He did?"

"Yep. 'Sharp Superstition'."

I remembered the painting – an acrylic montage of elements of every tradition that featured animal teeth as talismans or ritualistic artefacts, linked together with runes and tarot cards that referenced the animals concerned, or at least the traits those animals represented to the peoples concerned. I smiled. I could picture that painting in Tony's house. I knew he'd've hung it in the living room, above the sofa. There'd been a mirror there when I'd last visited – a mirror that was designed to be hung vertically, which had the space to be hung vertically, but which Tony had chosen to hang horizontally. Other than the small shaving mirror in the bathroom, it was the only reflective surface in the house. I'd hung the mirror on the vertical on a couple of occasions – it had always been returned to the horizontal. Tony never said anything about it.

"I hope he likes it." As I stepped out into the street, I held the door open for a couple in their late twenties, early thirties, smiling and touching in the way of a couple moving towards the next logical step in intimate relationships.

With a pang, I realised I'd never had that with Tony. Perhaps because I'd kept too much back from him.

Too much of the kind of trouble I was in now.

It had never been this bad, though. It had always been relatively tame stuff, grown up schoolboy naughtiness. This, though – this was bad.

I wished I could talk to Tony, even though I knew what he'd say. Since talking to Tony wasn't an option, I needed to find Al. Sooner rather than later.

Alexander

I don't know what I'd expected – the kind of interview room one sees in television police dramas, all drab grey, furniture bolted to the floor, knife marks on the table, ominous stains on the floor, and Big Brother watching from a high corner lest suspect or officers get a little frisky.

But, of course, I wasn't under arrest. I was here of my own free will, and, as such, I was shown up a set of concrete, institution grey stairs to a large, open plan office, with off white walls and thick grey cord carpet.

I hadn't expected a female officer, either. Especially not one who was prettily plump, with hair that fell down her back like a carpet of autumn leaves. Surely the police should make their female officers wear their hair in pony tails? Surely that would be more professional? And surely she should be wearing a suit, not the skirt in shades of green and gold with a black turtle-neck sweater that she was wearing? It was very distracting. Receptionists and secretaries were supposed to be attractively distracting. Police officers were not.

"Can I get you anything, Mr. Clifford-Alistair? Tea, coffee, some water?"

One of the things I'd always believed was that it was foolish to eat or drink anything in a police station. It was a ruse to get hold of your DNA. Before I'd become aware of what DNA was, and how it was harvested, I'd thought that the police would use food and drink to introduce truth drugs, or poison. I shook my head, smiling. Smiles allowed one to get away with a multitude of sins. "No, thank you." Quite apart from truth drugs, poison, and DNA harvesting, I strongly suspected that the teabags would be weak supermarket value, and the coffee would be the terrible, pound a jar instant. I wasn't about to suffer that particular indignity.

"Okay. So, I understand from my uniform colleagues that a group of individuals congregated outside your offices yesterday morning, and caused something of a disturbance?"

"They completely blocked the pavement. They weren't making

noise, as such, but they did seem to be rather... well, *threatening* seems too strong a word, but, well, I *was* somewhat...concerned by their behaviour. They seemed as though they were on the edge of something. Some kind of action that would have been...undesirable. Does that make sense?"

"Yes, absolutely." The attractive woman officer was making notes. She glanced up and smiled encouragingly. It struck me that human beings could probably communicate quite complexly through smiles. The range of smiles, and the meanings behind each of those smiles, suggests that smiles could actually replace language as a form of communication. "So, you were afraid of these people, would you say?"

"Not afraid, as such... more... sensibly wary."

"That makes sense. Did you notice any individual or individuals in particular?"

"There was a woman with short, red hair. She sort of seemed to be in charge, I suppose. I saw your uniformed officers speaking to her."

"Okay, I'll check back through the reports, and see what information we have on this woman. We will obviously want to talk to her further. Now, can you think what these people wanted to talk to you about?"

A broad, open, engaging smile. "I honestly don't know. I was given to understand that they had some issues with the returns on their investment portfolios, but, obviously, the very nature of investments is that they fluctuate. Clients are always fully informed of this before they commit."

"And these particular investments hadn't fluctuated more wildly, say, than you yourself, as an experienced professional, would expect?"

"Absolutely not. What you need to understand is that these are long-term investments – a minimum term of ten years, although many people choose to leave their investments in the fund for much longer. Certain of our funds do pay a monthly income, but it is made perfectly clear that this is not a fixed income. People shouldn't rely on it."

"And all of these individuals had these income-paying funds?"

"I don't know – I didn't speak with them."

"Well, don't worry – we'll be speaking with all of them, and, if they do all have the same fund, we might come back to you with a few more questions, if that's okay?"

I couldn't interpret the female officer's smile, this time, so I simply responded with an I've-nothing-to-hide one of my own, and handed her a business card. "Absolutely. My office and mobile numbers are on there, as are my work and personal emails. I can give you my landline number at home, too?"

"Please."

I took the card back briefly, scribbled my landline number on the reverse, and returned it. "Is that it?" A smile again: hopeful, eager, anxious to have been of help.

"For now, yes. I'll show you out." Another smile I couldn't read. This was beginning to worry me a little, even though I knew I was simply being paranoid. I wasn't a suspect. I wasn't under arrest. I was an upstanding citizen who had come to his local police station of his own free will.

There was no reason for the police to suspect anything at all.

Max

Come on, Al. Pick up. Pick up, dammit.
I drummed my knuckles on the deck of the boat as I listened to Al's phone ring out. I'd gone everywhere I could think of in Lothing, and no one had seen him.

 The phone cut to voicemail: "You have reached the offices of Eastern Rise Investments. We're sorry we're not available to take your call at this time, but if you'd like to leave your name, contact details, and a brief message, we'll get back to you as soon as we can."

Beeeeeeeeeep.
"Al, it's me. We need to talk. Sooner rather than later." I paced back and forth across the deck as the silence on the other end of the phone screamed in my ear. "Alex, dammit, this is important. Call me."

 I stabbed the phone off, and immediately clicked it back to life and began furiously typing, one handed, my other hand twisting and writhing through my hair. Gods, but this was an unmitigated fucking disaster. It wasn't supposed to be like this. It wasn't supposed to end like this. Nothing was meant to have been able to go wrong. It had all seemed so simple, so perfect, in the beginning.

 I'd seen the crowd outside Alex's office yesterday, and I'd known what they were there for. I'd taken the only action I could think of at the time – it hadn't been the right one, but it had, in reality, been the only one open to me.

 I wondered why Alex hadn't come back to the office yet, and, if he had, and I hadn't noticed, why he wasn't answering his phone. The offices were still dark, but that didn't mean he wasn't there, lying low. I just wished he'd answer his damn phone.

 This had been a crazy idea right from the start. I'd've seen that, if I hadn't been so focused on the chance to make some easy cash. I hated the fact that art paid pretty poorly, unless you somehow found superstardom, which happened to basically 0.001% of all artists ever.

I'd tried working in a the mainstream – advertising agencies, graphic designers, illustration – but I'd never been able to stick it for very long. Too many rules, too many meetings, too many talentless bimbos, of both sexes, trying to act like they were something special. Too much elevating creativity to some kind of sainthood.

Creativity wasn't a god, to be put on a pedestal and worshipped. It wasn't an aspiration. It simply *was*, the raw, wild part of all of us. Everyone had creativity in them – for too many people, though, it was shut down, shut away, shut up. Our inner children all have ADHD, and we can either help them find a fulfilling outlet for that energy and drive to do, see, feel, *be* more, or we can stifle them, and watch, helpless and handwringing, as they fall into one disaster after another, dragging us along with them.

I read the text message I'd been typing through:

ALEX, IT'S ME. WE NEED TO TALK. NOW. MEET ME AT THE USUAL PLACE, USUAL TIME.

I'd been told to throw a smokescreen over any communications with Alex, make it sound like legitimate business – I snorted at the idea that "legitimate business" meant the individual conducting said business was automatically law-abiding: some of the biggest crooks I've known have done everything on the up and up, with the approval of society, as pillars of their communities.

I glanced at my watch. Two-thirty. Another three and a half hours until I needed to be waiting for Alexander Clifford-Alistair. I just hoped he showed up. Because if he didn't, things could get very messy, very quickly.

P.C. Feroc Hanson
LB 599

"So, what sort of art does this Max do, then? I mean, painting, obviously – the easel and canvases sort of gave that away – but what kind of paintings?"

"The one in the living room's one of his."

"The tribal artefacts one, with the runes and tarot cards?"

"Yeah. He had an exhibition in the summer, down at The Banana Lounge."

"That was Max's work? You didn't say."

"Didn't seem relevant."

"Why didn't I realise? He must have had a poster up, a bio, something like that?"

Tony shook his head. "No. That's not how Max plays. He goes for the mystique. His profiles all simply refer to him as "the artist." No names, no pack drill."

Tony raised another forkful of food to his mouth, and I suddenly processed what he was eating.

"Is that – salad?"

"Yes. You don't need to sound quite so surprised. I've eaten it at home before, I'm sure I have."

"Not without dressing on, you haven't."

"That's because you automatically put dressing on salad."

"Salad is *meant* to have dressing."

"I happen to like naked salad."

I gave Tony a pointed look, one eyebrow raised. I wasn't nearly as good at that gesture as he was.

"You don't need to give me that look, either – you might have noticed that I drink diet coke, too."

"Yeah, and I remember expressing my feeling of deep and bitter irony at that, too. If you're capable of some healthy attitudes, why can't you be consistently healthy?"

Tony grinned.

"Because then what would you have to criticise?"

I took a long gulp of mineral water. "Look, Tony..." I glanced around nervously. Walls have ears, especially in the nick. "Have you written up your report on Max's break in yet?"

"No. I've got my basic notes, but I haven't had a chance to write them up. The Sarge has been on my back about it. So don't start, please. I'll do it now, while it's quiet. I've still got the piece of nonsense with Laura at the bank to write up as well."

I sighed. "I'll talk to Aimee, see if we can get off watch for an hour or so so you can get your notes sorted."

"She'll just assign you to another unit. And I'll be bored and headachey on my own, shut up in here when I should be out on the streets. *My* streets."

"I'll tell her we both need to write up our notes."

"She'll never believe it of you – you're the Force's golden boy."

"So why'd they pair me with the black sheep, then?"

Tony grinned, and took a long, slow draught of coffee. "Hoping that you'd be a good influence on me, I expect."

I gave a wry laugh. "Well, they're shit out of luck on that one, aren't they?"

"Always happens this way around. They never learn. The Force thrives on its bad boys. Bringing in mandatory degrees is going to destroy us." He looked up. "Why're you asking about Max's break in reports, anyway?"

I lowered my voice. "Because we really need to talk, quite seriously, about whether he could be involved in Angela Dalloway's burglary."

"Feroc, we've been through this -"

"No. *You've* been through it, and you've admitted you have a conflict of interest. Tony, you said yourself you've turned a blind eye to things in the past. Don't keep doing that now."

"Look, I don't love Max. Probably never did. Alright? But that doesn't mean I want to see him take a fall, okay?"

"Tony..." I sighed, and rubbed a hand over my eyes. "You'd make the perfect straight bloke, you know that?"

"What're you on about now?"

"When you care for someone, even if you don't love them, you have an overwhelming drive to protect them from life's unpleasantness. It's how straight guys are with women, usually because their inherent sexism means they don't believe women are capable of handling unpleasantness."

"What's wrong with that? What's wrong with wanting to make a bloody hard life a little less painful for some poor sod?"

"Because it holds them back, Tony. It holds them back from realising that their actions have consequences, and that they need to be responsible for their own behaviour. In the short-term, yes, it makes life easier for them. In the long run?" I shook my head sadly. "It damages them, Tony."

He got up, deliberately not looking at me.

"Not as much as always being made to take the rap for everything that happened, whether you could help it or not, whether it was your fault or not."

"Tony -"

"What?"

The wildness, the fury, was back. But something was different, this time. This time, I wasn't afraid.

"Tony: if you make life easier for Max, now, you make it harder for yourself. If you make life harder for yourself, you make it harder for me. Max isn't part of your life in that way any more, Tony. But I am. Who matters more, Tony? The guy who walked away, or the guy who was there when you were bleeding out on the floor of the Heart of Darkness? The guy who gave you a lifestyle, or the guy who would gladly give you his life?"

I stood upright, head raised, shoulders set, managing to shake only on the inside. The whole canteen was silent, watching, waiting.

"I don't even know how you could ask me that." Tony's voice was a howl of anguish, pain, and real, genuine hurt. But he wasn't yet destroyed. The edge of his anger still shone through. I stepped forward, and stepped up.

"What's more important is that you want answer. What matters most, Tony? Your past, or your future?"

The silence was deafening. It seemed to echo through eternity like the sound of a cell door slamming shut.

"Damn you, Feroc. Damn you."

"No. Damn Max – he's the one who's making you choose. Not me."

"You're the one standing there."

"Yeah? You should read the Christian bible sometime, Tony – the guys who're standing in the gap are never the ones who've done anything wrong."

"I'll talk to Max."

"No. You won't. You'll talk to CID. Or I will – and you can imagine how that's going to look for you."

"Are you blackmailing me?"

I swallowed, almost choking on the dryness of my throat. But I gave answer to the challenge.

"No." My voice was quiet, soft. A caress. A lover's whisper. "I'm reminding you that you are duty bound to move forward, to embrace the future, and all it brings, with all of your soul."

"And to honour the past."

"To honour, yes – but not to remain ensnared by. I have the power to destroy your future, and leave you with the ashes of a past you can't go back to. You know that – it's why you're angry, still. You recognise my power, and it calls to your own. But your power is chained by the memory of something you only thought you had. You can't act, Tony, because you are not in full possession of your power."

I closed my eyes, waiting for the blow.

"I'll talk to CID. Not now – I can't do it just yet – but soon. Today. And Feroc?"

I opened my eyes. "Yes?"

"I will always choose you. I don't even need to know what the other choices are. It's always you. Even when I hate you with every fibre and thought in me, I love you. Never, ever doubt that. Never, ever doubt *me*."

Nothing is ever louder than the sound of brazen eavesdroppers pretending they hadn't been focused on you and your conversation.

Alexander

Just as we approached the first-floor landing, my phone beeped twice. I'd taken it off silent when I'd stood up to leave. I tried to ignore it.

"You should probably check that, Mr. Clifford-Alistair. It might be a client trying to get in touch with you."

"Yes..." I felt the woman officer's eyes on me, the way a man would never have dared to look at me. I'd been going to wait until I was outside, away from this place, to check the inevitable text message, but that, apparently, wasn't going to be an option.

I flipped open my jacket, and pulled my phone out of the inside pocket. I stared at the screen, feeling suddenly sick.

"Is everything okay, sir?"

"Ah, yes...well, no, yes, yes, everything's fine. Just, ahhh, one of my staff. They, um, needed clarification on something. I should, ah, probably get back to the office." God, I sounded like an idiot, blithering away with all those ahs and ums. Worse: I sounded like I had something to hide, which is most definitely *not* what one wants to do in front of the officers of the law.

Quickly, I typed back:

OK. DON'T CALL ME.

I wondered why the hell he'd chosen to ignore that long-standing rule. I'd explained its importance enough times, for pity's sake! What was *wrong* with the man?

I pocketed the phone, and gave an apologetic smile. "Sorry about that. He's fairly new, still a little bit anxious about things. Not quite found his feet yet."

"Don't worry – I completely understand. We've all been there, and I'm sure, in a sector such as yours, its far better for people to ask stupid questions than make stupid – and costly – mistakes."

"Oh, absolutely."

"We didn't get round to talking in detail about what it is your company actually offer, did we?" Her smile seemed genuine, but there was something off about it. Nevertheless, I returned it with a bright, glowing one of my own, and, setting my briefcase on the floor, opened it and pulled out a brochure.

"Here; it should all be in fairly straightforward English, everything's set out, all the funds we manage, the predicted returns. There's a registration form at the back, and contributions can start from as little as a hundred pounds, in our smaller funds." She nodded, flicking through the brochure. "Really? That's quite good – so many of these places you have to have at least five thousand just to walk through their doors."

"Oh, I know. At Eastern Rise Investments, we very much believe that *everyone*, no matter what their income level, should be able to benefit from quality, professional, financial management and advice."

"Absolutely. So many people are struggling to keep a decent amount of savings set aside for a rainy day, when they really don't need to be. And younger people, entering the workforce for the first time, are utterly clueless about pensions and the like."

"I'm so glad to see that there are some people outside of my sector who see such things as important. It very much validates my work, really."

"Indeed. One thing I am curious about though, Mr. Clifford-Alistair: I can see that it is clearly explained that the value of individual and corporate investments can fall as well as rise – you actually repeat that several times, using different phrasing each time, which is good practice – and yet still, a relatively large group of people were upset enough at the reports they received, were anxious enough about what was going on at your company, to turn up outside your door yesterday morning. That suggests they'd tried the more usual methods of communicating with professionals such as yourself – telephone and email – and had either been ignored outright, or given a brush off. Neither of which are very professional, really. Are they, Mr. Clifford-Alistair?"

Shit, I thought. *This really wasn't going according to plan.*

"Look, I really do -"

"Didn't you just send a text to your staff member? Surely you were able to give at least brief clarification?"

"Well, yes, but -"

"I'm surprised you think clarifying something for a staff member who could easily ask a more senior colleague is more important than helping us clear up exactly what's been going on, why clients of yours are suddenly blocking public thoroughfares and making a general nuisance of themselves. I mean, it can't do the reputation of Eastern Rise Investments much good to have the police round, can it?"

"Look -"

"No, Mr. Clifford-Alistair. *You* look. You left it too late, today: the red-haired woman you mentioned, Ms. Ravenswood? She came in first thing this morning. And what *she* had to say about your company, and one of your schemes in particular, was *very* interesting indeed."

"She's paranoid – I've had to instruct my staff not to take her calls -"

"But you'll still take her money?"

"It's not hers – it's a pension fund she manages."

"Indeed. And people who manage company pension funds, even relatively small ones, don't tend to be given to emotional volatility. They tend to understand the swings and roundabouts nature of the stock market, and investment generally, quite well, wouldn't you say?"

"Well, yes, usually, but -"

"But you don't want to say so in Ms. Ravenswood's case. Because if you acknowledged that she was a fairly intelligent, level-headed woman, then it calls your company into question rather sharply, doesn't it?"

"Look, I won't stand for this sort of slander! I have to get back to my office now."

I started to step forward, but the female officer was suddenly in front of me.

"You know what I think, Mr. Clifford-Alistair? I think Ms. Ravenswood is right – that something very dodgy is going on at

Eastern Rise Investments, and especially with one particular fund, which, interestingly enough, every single one of the people outside your offices yesterday has money invested in – the 'Avin an Art Attack' fund. Now, perhaps you'd like to come back into the office, and talk me through exactly how that fund works? Or, rather, how it is *supposed* to work, since Ms. Ravenswood very eruditely explained the ways in which it appears to *not* be working as outlined in your literature, on your website, and, indeed, in the agreements your company has with clients of that particular fund."

"Look, this is harassment! I need to get back to my office – I have important business that isn't getting done while you're keeping me here! My staff need a guiding hand, a managerial presence -"

"Why would that be? Surely you've recruited well, and provided sufficient training? Your staff know how to get on with their respective roles without you peering over their shoulder, surely?" She'd taken out her own mobile phone while she'd been talking. I'd been puzzled at first, then, with dawning horror, I realised what she was doing.

As she held the phone up to her ear, but angled slightly towards me, I heard the unmistakable tone of a phone ringing in an empty room. Then my own voice:

"You have reached the offices of Eastern Rise Investments. We're sorry there is no one available to take your call at the moment: if you'd like to leave your name, contact details, and a brief message, we'll get back to you as soon as we can. Thank you."

Beeeeeeppppp.

"Oh dear, Mr. Clifford-Alistair. It seems you really can't find the staff these days – everyone seems to have gone home. I'd give them a stern talking to in the morning, if I were you. It's -" she glanced at her watch "- just about three-thirty. Do you employ flexi-time working at your offices, Mr. Clifford-Alistair?"

I grimaced. "No."

"No. I didn't think so. The interesting thing is, Mr. Clifford-Alistair, I did a quick background check on your company, when my colleagues in uniform first dropped their report on my desk. Standard procedure, helps us know who we're dealing with. And you don't seem to employ *anyone*, Mr. Clifford-Alistair. Apart from a Mr. Parker-James, who is listed as a "retained consultant." Now, do you want to know something interesting about Mr. Parker-James?"

"What?"

"Perhaps we should sit down in my office. This may come as a bit of a shock to you."

Having seemingly no choice, I meekly followed her back into the room I'd thought I'd escaped. Like a lamb to the slaughter. Although it still wasn't a formal interview room. There was still hope.

I sat down, and the female officer perched on the edge of the desk, a mannish affectation that quite set my teeth on edge.

"You see, " she began, conversationally, as though we were discussing potential holiday destinations, or the weather, "Mr. Parker-James has something of a chequered past in the financial services sector -"

"Andrew is still relatively young – he's not yet forty. He started a business off his own bat, Ms... Fraud, was it?"

"Freud. Detective Constable Freud. Like the psychoanalyst."

"My apologies. Ms. Freud. As I was saying, he started his own business, which he built into a prestigious, award-winning company -"

"He was fined for mismanagement of cases. Missing Court-appointed filing dates. Mishandling of funds. Lack of adequate training and supervision of staff. His turn over for administration clerks is shocking. Usually, financial services admin, particularly in insolvency, are fairly stable, settled individuals."

"He had a run of bad hires. A junior manager was given responsibility for making hiring decisions when she perhaps wasn't quite ready. If you looked into things thoroughly, you'd find, in fact, that in one case the dismissal of the individual in question was for reasons that were quite beyond anything Andrew could have anticipated, or been expected to rectify. You see, that young man -"

"Had schizophrenia, which he hadn't disclosed, as he had previously been in receipt of Job Seekers' Allowance, and was presumably trying to avoid anything that might cause a prospective employer to refuse him employment, and an inevitable sanction from the Department of Work and Pensions. Your 'consultant' had the poor guy sacked for gross misconduct. He'll probably never work again, and certainly not in financial services."

"Which, all things considered, is probably for the best."

"Really? Best for whom? Rohan Hunter? That's his name, by the way. The guy who's future your pal Andrew ruined. He was barely twenty-five, Mr. Clifford-Alistair. Trying to rebuild his life following a devastating mental health diagnosis, and several years of unemployment as a result of the difficulties associated with being an undiagnosed – and thus unmedicated – schizophrenic, within a framework that is notoriously unsympathetic to the people it is supposed to be helping. Was it best for him? Or perhaps you mean it was best for the taxpayer, who is presumably supporting Mr. Hunter in his re-acquaintance with unemployment? Or perhaps it was best for all the other people out there living with a diagnosis of schizophrenia, who, if they come across Rohan Hunter, will be faced with the fact that no one wants them? That they're broken. Useless. Scum. That the business community doesn't see them as deserving of employment, of an income, of independence. Perhaps it was best for those peoples' families, robbed of hope for their loved ones' futures? Perhaps it was best for the NHS, whose psychiatrists are now going to have to return to intensively supporting Rohan Hunter, when, by all accounts, he was at minimal contact because of the amount of improvement he'd made. Mostly related to finally hearing "Yes" from a prospective employer?" She turned to face me, her eyes bright with a chilling fire. "Or maybe, Mr. Clifford-Alistair, it was just best for your pal Andrew's personal prejudices?"

"Look, employers aren't a kind of social service: businesses are here to make a profit, not to mop up society's overspill."

"Overspill? Is that what you consider people with health issues, Mr. Clifford-Alistair? Not really human? Just a problem to be shifted somewhere else, out of sight? Something for someone else to deal with?"

"No, look, I didn't say that -"

"But you did. You used the word 'overspill', quite deliberately. And what about the other people who were sacked from your pal's firm, Parker Devereux? Did they all have mental health issues, too? Were they all 'overspill'? What about those who chose to move on, before they'd advanced in their career?"

"Look, I can't tell you anything much about Parker Devereux. That was Andrew's firm."

"Indeed. 'Was.' Past tense. He was forced to hand over the running of Parker Devereux to his business partner, Lionel Devereux, wasn't he? And several people left at about that time – people who'd been close to, loyal to, Andrew Parker-James. And his most recent venture -" she flicked through her notepad "- Business Trending, doesn't seem to be having quite the same meteoric rise as did Parker-Devereux."

"Business Trending is a completely different premise -"

"Still, I'd expect the trade press to have had *something* to say about it. But there's been nothing. Financial services is a small world, and the consultancy firms that specialise in that sector tend to have quite a strong reputation. Business Trending seems to have sunk without trace – just a few ripples when they release their quarterly returns. Which are not exactly earth-shattering."

"It's still a young business -"

"Run by a manager who doesn't seem to know what he's doing, and, from the reports of his warnings when he was with Parker-Devereux – who, interestingly, have completely changed their name, and have issued a couple of statements, in both the trade and general press, to the effect that they are no longer associated with Andrew Parker-James – was quite assiduously focused on not doing very much, and delegating work that he should have been attending to personally to underqualified, underskilled, untrained admin staff. Who were already dealing with an average of sixty-three cases each, when the industry best practice guidelines suggest a maximum caseload of forty to fifty. And that's for an experienced administrator."

"Look, when you're building a brand -"

"Is when it's most important to get things right. To invest in training and developing your people. To not abdicate responsibility, and only bother with the glamorous side of things – courting clients, giving Press statements, addressing the Chamber of Commerce."

I slumped back in my uncomfortable seat. "Look, I don't know what you think the unfortunate experiences at Parker-Devereux have to do with Eastern Rise, but -"

"I think the fact that you have a glory-hunting, widely discredited individual listed as the only person associated with your company in anything remotely resembling a staff member capacity has everything to do with an unhappy mob gathering at your gates. Now, shall I take you on a little stroll through Ms. Ravenswood's statement, given to myself this morning, and enhanced in places with my own research, with sources credited appropriately, so you can be rest assured I haven't just taken a hatchet piece in the red-tops, or a disgruntled Wikipedia article, as Gospel truth? And perhaps you can point out ways in which certain things could be seen differently? Suggest some new angles?"

I glanced at my watch. It was already nearly four p.m. I sighed. "I don't suppose I have a choice, do I?"

The female officer smiled. It was a shark's grin, all teeth and no solace.

"Not really. Alexander Clifford-Alistair, I'm arresting you on suspicion of embezzlement. You do not have to say anything, but anything you do say will be taken down, and may be used in evidence against you should your case be heard before a Court of law. Do you understand these rights, as I have read them to you?"

"Let's get on with this, shall we?"

"I'll take that as a yes. Move."

Brynn

I was anxious, stroking the crushed velvet of the sofa I'd upcycled and reupholstered myself, back when I'd been in my twenties, before either of the terms became fashionable. I wanted to get up and start pacing the room – I felt restless, out of sorts – but it was important that I learned to control disruptive impulses.

The good thing was, I knew *why* I was anxious: inevitably, in whatever form it took with them, the police of Lothing would be preparing to act on the information I had provided to them this morning.

I'd never reported anyone to the police before, even though I'd been in plenty of situations where doing so would have been the "right" course of action. Mainly people who clearly couldn't handle the recreational drugs everyone took when I was a student, but also, more recently, people engaged in anti-social behaviour, and someone whom I knew to be involved in blackmailing prominent businesspeople. I couldn't have explained why I didn't report that particular individual – I suppose I thought he had enough going on, without a criminal record making it worse. Besides, he was improving, in terms of his sophistication, and I knew he wouldn't actually cause anyone harm. If he didn't get paid, he didn't become violent. None of his threats were physical, as far as I knew, and none of them were against people.

So, having established myself as a tolerant, bleeding-heart liberal, why did I decide to present the police with sufficient evidence to arrest and question Alexander Clifford-Alistair? Perhaps because, unlike the other criminals I've known, who were either young and foolish, or dealing with other problems that no one had any intention of supporting them through, Clifford-Alistair had everything. A comfortable lifestyle, devoted-seeming, if somewhat brainless, wife, two darling daughters who doubtless fawned over Daddy, a successful business, financial wealth, respect, and yet was still reaching out and snatching more and more and more. Unlike those others I'd known, he had no reason for his behaviours, and no need of their rewards. It was that that damned him, in the end: the needlessness of it all. The pure greed that he didn't even bother to hide.

I'd got up at seven, as I usually did, whether it was a work day or not, made myself a cup of tea, and, when the morning paper had arrived at quarter past seven, sat and read it in the kitchen. I'd showered, dressed in my usual business suit, a blue so pale it was almost grey, which I'd paired with a gold blouse, and blush pink pearl earrings.

At eight o'clock, feeling somewhat nervous, I'd headed out of the door. Lothing police station was only a ten minute walk from my flat, if I went directly, but I needed to spend some time by the sea, first. I found the waves calming – especially, interestingly enough, when they themselves were least calm. October onwards was a good time for wild, restless weather – and, I suspected, for wild, restless souls.

In the end, I was almost late, and had to pause on the neat path that led to the automatic doors, in order to take a few deep breaths.

"Can I help you, madam?"

"Yes – I was involved in a … well, in a situation, yesterday. Uniformed officers attended, and I said I'd pop in to speak to someone from CID today."

"Right. Can I take your name?"

"Brynn Ravenswood."

"And what was the nature of the incident?"

"I was part of a group of people who had assembled outside the offices of Eastern Rise Investments Ltd, at Waveney Court on Chambers Road. The uniformed officers who attended were P.Cs Hanson and Raglan."

"Okay, I'll just see if anyone's free to talk to you. If you'd like to take a seat?"

I looked around, and chose a seat against the back wall. The wall adjacent to the doors was taken up with a woman officer talking soothingly to a distressed-seeming elderly lady, who kept talking about how her brother had dropped her off in Oxford Street, and she was supposed to meet him somewhere so that they could go for lunch together, but she couldn't remember where she was meant to meet him, and she mustn't keep him waiting as he didn't like hanging about in central London, because the street parking meters were so expensive. Alzheimer's, clearly: the poor lady had got herself lost, and the only memory she could access was a time – a happier time, perhaps when she had been younger, and more hopeful – when she had visited London with her brother, and gone shopping in Oxford Street. I'd found myself wondering about that visit: What did she think of London, of all those shops? Did she buy anything, or merely wish for things? Where had her brother taken her for lunch? What kind of car did he drive, back then?

"I was ever so cross with him this morning, y'see. I quite lost my temper. I hope he's not angry when I find him."

"I'm sure he won't be, Beverley. Now, there's a name here, and a telephone number – Eve. Does that mean anything to you?" The old woman's face had brightened: she'd looked almost like a girl again. "My little girl. My beautiful baby girl. They said she was going to be a boy, see, and we were going to call him Adam – that was my maiden name, see, Adamson. Myrtle and Geoffrey Adamson. But anyway, Adam was a girl, so we called him Eve. She was so beautiful. Such a perfect little baby, and she never cried, not once, she didn't. A good, quiet little girl." I'd smiled at the blending of genders. I'd hoped Eve was at home, that she could come and get her mother, and that everything would be alright.

"Okay, what we'll do is, I'll take you through the doors just there, where it's a bit warmer, make you a nice cup of tea, and you can chat to my colleague, Garth – he's a handsome young man, you'll like him – while I see if I can get Eve on the telephone for you." The old woman frowned. "We're not on the telephone, dear. And Eve's just a baby. She can't hardly speak, yet."

"Well, we'll see if there's anyone at this number who can help. If you come along with me now, I'll get you a nice cup of tea."

"I like tea. Arthur always makes me a cup of tea in the morning."

"Is that your husband?"

"Arthur. He lives in the house with me, and makes me tea in the morning."

"Okay. Here we go."
I'd watched them walk past the young man who was slumped,
head down, in the row of chairs beside a set of double doors that
I'd assumed led into the police station proper. His jeans had been
at least a size too large, and not in the fashionable sense. His shirt
had seemed a little tight across his broad shoulders.
 He'd lifted his head, and looked at me: his eyes had seemed full
of hopeless despair, and it had hurt me to look at him.
 The man on the desk had called over. "Mr. Hunter?" The young
man had looked up, suddenly eager, only to be greeted by a slow
headshake.
 "There's no one about who can help you just at the moment. It's a
little early still. D'you want to come back this afternoon, maybe?
Say around three, four o'clock?"
 The young man had got to his feet in a surprisingly fluid
movement. "What's the point? There won't be anyone who can
help then, either. All there'll be as an ambulance, waiting to drive
me God knows how many miles away. As soon as I told you about
the schizophrenia, you made up your mind you weren't going to
deal with me. Well, I'm not going back to hospital. No way."
 He'd left before the man on the desk could answer his
accusations: he'd walked out with a strange kind of startling pride.
Tall. Strong. Defiant. As I had with the elderly woman, I'd found
myself hoping he would be alright.
 The man on the desk had shaken his head, smiling in my
direction. "No helping some people." I'd smiled back, not wanting
to say anything, and he'd headed off, presumably to try and find
someone to deal with me.
 I'd felt a strange sense of unease: everyone always talked about
how hard the elderly had it, how much discrimination they
suffered, and how men of all ages were so much more privileged
than women of any age, and yet that poor young man had been
ignored, made to feel worthless, while the elderly lady was
cosseted and helped to the utmost limits of peoples' ability. I
hadn't liked the conclusions that had begun to form in the shadows
of my mind.

"Brynn?"

I'd been startled, lost in thought, and suddenly jolted back to reality.

"Yes?" I'd stood up, taken a tentative step forward.

The woman – I'd guessed her to be in her early thirties – had held out a hand. "Hi. I'm D.C. Freud. Call me Tam. If you'd like to follow me? I can grab you a coffee on the way? Or tea?"

"No, I'm fine, thank you."

"If you're sure."

"Thank you, yes."

As I'd walked behind her, I'd noted the detective's style with approval. I loved the way the fabrics and colours of her skirt were arranged so that the skirt itself almost seemed to be alive, constantly shifting between states and thoughts. Her boots, which came to mid-shin, and collapsed down at the back, were a distressed black, its fade drawing attention away from them, focusing it on the skirt, and the semi-fitted, onyx-dark turtleneck that she wore.

Her hair had reminded me of a bonfire on an autumn evening, just as the sun was setting. There were endless shades and streaks and shadows to it, and, like the skirt, it seemed almost alive, as though at any moment it might spring off of her head and start a dance.

"Here we are." I'd followed her into a large, open plan office, which had, at first glance, seemed purely business. A second glance, however, had revealed small personal messages, hints at personality: A man's sweater in bright, vibrant purple draped over a chair. A plant, potted in an oversized cup and saucer, which were patterned in navy blue with pink polka dots. The tops of a couple of photo frames, one wooden, one sleek, curved glass, on different desks.

People had been standing, sitting, moving, talking. I'd wanted to take out my phone, snap a picture of this scene, so I could paint it later. But I'd realised that would be inappropriate – my memory would have to do.

"So, what can I help you with?"

I'd swallowed. "I think it's more what *I* can help *you* with. I assume you know about the, ah, the incident at Waveney Court yesterday?"

 The detective had smiled, nodding encouragingly. "Yes, The uniformed officers gave me a report. What was it all about?"

I'd come prepared for this question – it was a rather obvious one. I handed over the folder that I'd been clutching.

"I think you'll find it easier to read this first. Everything is in there, from the very beginning, right up until most recently. It's emails and letters between myself and Mr. Clifford-Alistair, of Eastern Rise Investments, concerning monies currently being managed by Eastern Rise, through their 'Avin' an Art Attack scheme, on behalf of the company pension fund for the Mythos Gallery in Southwold, a pension fund for which I am responsible. After failing to get any sort of response to my queries regarding the scheme's sudden drop in performance, I put several posts on social media, asking if anyone else had experienced falling revenues from the 'Avin' an Art Attack scheme. You see, that scheme is not actually linked to any of the financial markets, and should, therefore, provide a steady rate of return month on month."

"Is this draw-down income?"

"Oh, no. Nothing quite so handsome as that. No, the monthly amounts themselves are relatively small, but the scheme is intended to run for a minimum term of ten years, and of course, over that time, the returns would combine to represent a substantial return on investment."

"So, what happens at the end of ten years?"

"You're given the option to either cash in the fund, or to invest the lump sum in a managed portfolio, which focuses on ethical and cultural investments, both in the UK and overseas."

"I see. So for ten years, you're supposed to get a regular monthly return?"

"Yes – the scheme capital is used to provide loans to emerging artists, which they repay over a ten year period, with interest attached. Eastern Rise Investments keeps forty percent of the interest payments each month, and the remaining sixty percent is passed on to the various investors. I was very excited when I heard about the scheme, as it's exactly the sort of thing Mythos Gallery is keen to enact, and ten years is a fairly reasonable amount of time for an artist to begin to regularly make a name for themselves – and to regularly make a viable income, of course."

"Quite. But you noticed that the monthly returns had begun to change – when was that, exactly?"

"About four months ago. Obviously, I emailed Eastern Rise immediately, asking for clarification."

"And what was their response?"

"Silence. I then emailed Mr. Clifford-Alistair directly, again, receiving no response. I wrote letters, which I posted special delivery, and which were signed for, and I telephoned. My calls went unanswered. I would phone on different days, at different times of the day, but never receive an answer. One day, I phoned from my mother's house – the phone *was* answered then. Other investors in the 'Avin' an Art Attack scheme reported similar experiences, which suggests that any numbers held on file for scheme investors are deliberately being ignored."

"Hmm. Yes, that does seem a plausible explanation." The detective had tapped the folder with the tip of a pencil, and looked up at me.

"Are you willing to make a formal accusation against Mr. Clifford-Alistair?"

"Well...I mean, I don't know exactly what crime he's committed -"

"Don't worry. We'll sort all of that out. But you sincerely believe he is guilty of deliberate wrongdoing?"

"Yes. Absolutely."

"This couldn't be negligence on his part?"

"I don't see how, no. Not so consistently."

"Okay then – if you'd like to come back downstairs with me, I'll take you to a formal interview room, and we'll get a record of your statement, okay?"

I'd nodded, feeling dizzy with adrenaline. "Yes. Yes, that's fine."

It wasn't, of course – making a complaint to the police, however legitimate and necessary, is never "fine." But I supposed what I meant was *I* was fine about the process.

The interview room had looked exactly like what you see on TV, stark, aggressively utilitarian furniture, a bank of recording equipment on the back wall. Even here, under intimate and immediate observation, people had expressed themselves, their frustration, their displeasure. Their innocence, in one case. I'd imagined Alexander Clifford-Alistair in a room like this. Then pictured him in a cell. I'd doubted very much that he would be able to hold his composure for long. He was the kind of man that needed to have an audience. It's why the lack of obvious employees at Eastern Rise Investments was puzzling. I would have thought he would have wanted a crowd around him.

"Okay, so, what I'm going to do is ask you to tell me exactly what you believe Mr. Clifford-Alistair has done wrong, in your own words, and what reasons you have to believe this, again, in your own words. We'll be recording this, and I'll be writing down exactly what you say. When we're finished, you'll be able to read through what I've written, and I'll ask you to sign to say you agree with it. Does that make sense?"

I'd nodded. "What will happen to Mr. Clifford-Alistair? After this, I mean? After I've...given you my statement?"

"He'll be brought in for questioning in the matter, to give his version of events, if you like. As there's already been an incident at his premises requiring police contact, we'll give him twenty-four hours to present himself of his own volition, to discuss that matter, and, during those discussions, we'll put your accusations to him, and give him an opportunity to respond."

"What if he doesn't come in?"

"Then officers will go to his home and his place of work, and bring him here under caution."

"And after that?"

She'd given a rueful smile, and a slight shrug. "After that, it's up to the CPS – the Crown Prosecution Service – as to what, if anything, he'll be charged with. Whatever happens, whether this goes to Court or not, the fact that there has been a police

investigation into a complaint received will mean that the
Financial Conduct Authority will launch their own investigation."
I'd nodded. "Yes. I was aware of that."
"So – are you okay to start?"
I'd nodded. And it had begun – the end, that is.

 And now, I was sitting on a sofa that was as much an expression
of my personality, my hopes, my ambition, my dreams – which
were still unfulfilled, nearly fifteen years on – as it was an item of
furniture, worrying about the future of a man who, it seemed, had
only ever worried about himself.
 I got up, and headed to the kitchen. Tea, I decided. That was what
I needed: a nice, strong, sweet cup of tea. Even when you don't
like a person very much, contemplating their downfall is a
harrowing experience.

D.C. Tam Freud

"Got a cell spare for this one, Sarge?"

Aimee Gardner looked up from her computer screen. "Oh, I'm sure we can find him somewhere. Nice locked door, his own bed, not much of a view, sadly, but you can't have everything. What's he in for?"

"Suspicion of embezzlement, in relation to third party funds under management."

"Name?" Aimee Gardner looked at Clifford-Alistair, and I saw his expression of distaste. Obviously not a man to extend the hand of welcome to women, or to what he no doubt thought of as "Our coloured brethren."

"Alexander Clifford-Alistair. It's hyphenated. That *is* relevant, and important."

Aimee Gardner hadn't missed the expression on Clifford-Alistair's face. "Alex-hyphen-ander... Ooops, silly me. Of course, you meant the *surname* is hyphenated. Sorry about that." She typed, not looking up. "Address?" Clifford-Alistair gave his address in a voice that carried tightly-leashed frustration. A couple of hours in a cell should take care of that.

"Date of birth?"

"Thirteenth of September Nineteen-Sixty-Seven."

A year after England won the World Cup. I bet he was permanently aggrieved about that. No doubt if he were a year older, he'd've found some way to claim that England's World Cup win was somehow connected to his approaching birth.

"Any health issues we should know about? Any medications you're taking?"

"No."

"Is there anyone you'd like informed of your arrest?"

"No. I see no reason to trouble my wife with this nonsense."

"Would you like a solicitor present?"

"No. I've done nothing wrong – why would I need a solicitor?"

"You are entitled to change your mind about having a solicitor present at any time. Do you understand?"

"Yes, of course. But I won't need a solicitor."

"I'm making a note that you've waived your right to legal representation. As I've already said, you are entitled to request a solicitor at any point. Empty your pockets, please."

Alexander Clifford-Alistair's pockets were unremarkable. The latest smartphone. A wallet made of leather that looked far softer than anything I'd ever owned. A packet of cigarettes – Mayfair – and a silver lighter, engraved with the initials *ACA*. At least we could be reasonably certain he wasn't a common thief.

"Remove your watch and belt, please."

"*What?!*"

"Please take off your watch and your belt, and place them on the desk."

"You can't do this! I want a male officer here, right now!"

Aimee Gardner stood up, stretched, and looked around, like a cat scouting for its next plaything.

Suddenly, she smiled. "Tony!"

"Sarge?" Tony Raglan, who'd looked as though he and Feroc Hanson had been heading up to CID, paused, and sauntered over to the desk. He glanced at me, and something unreadable came into his eyes.

"Mr. Clifford-Alistair has come over all shy about taking off his belt and his watch. He wants a male officer present."

Tony turned, the professional smile that senior officers quickly learned to fear and distrust in equal measure spread across his face.

"Well, here I am, Mr. Clifford-Alistair. A male officer, as requested. Now, do as the Sergeant says, and take off your belt and wristwatch."

"This is preposterous!"

"No, sir – this is protocol."

Turning to Aimee Gardner, Tony asked,

"So – who's his brief?"

"Waived. Says he doesn't need one, because he's innocent."

"Oh for a life where everyone who walked through these hallowed halls took that view." Tony turned back to Clifford-Alistair.

"Haven't you got your belt and watch off yet? Come on, man. Stop mucking about."

"I'll have your jobs for this. All of you."

Tony grinned. "I think my uniform might be a bit loose on you, sir. Good lad – see, that wasn't hard, was it?"

Alexander Clifford-Alistair glared. Aimee Gardner handed Tony a set of keys. "Since he seems to like you, you can escort him to the Presidential Suite, otherwise known, in common parlance, as cell three."

"Who's in one and two?"

"Our old friend Haribo is in cell one, the usual, and cell two is a D&D."

"At this time of day?"

"Yup. That's Lothing for you."

"Yeah – but they all go off to Norwich, and howl about the Prince of Wales. This way, Mr. Clifford-Alistair."

"I shall be making a formal complaint about this. And suing your station, and you, personally, for false imprisonment."

Tony grinned at me and Aimee over his shoulder. "Don't you love it when you get the ones who know big words?"

"Absolutely." Aimee Gardner's response dripped with sarcasm.

"Right – shoes off."

"My *shoes?*"

"Well, I'd hardly ask you to take mine off, would I? And yes, shoes usually does mean shoes. The things on your feet."

Tony opened the side hatch. "In here, please."

"This is beyond a joke."

"In you go. You can think about what you want to say in your letter of complaint." Tony closed the hatch on Clifford-Alistair's shoes – certainly the best-looking footwear Lothing nick had seen in a long while – and led the man himself into the cell. "Bed. Toilet in the corner. There's four sheets of toilet paper. If you want any more than that, you'll have to press the buzzer beside the door. Someone'll come as soon as they're not busy. It might take a while. You've missed lunch, but dinner's in an hour. Any special requests? By which I mean do you require halal, kosher, vegan, or

115

vegetarian food, or can we chuck you any old muck?"

"I won't be treated like this."

"No special dietary requirements. Got that, Sarge?"

"Yep. Not religious, not a snowflake, not vegetarian. Nice and simple, just the way I like them."

Tony locked the cell door, and made his way back to the custody desk, handing over the keys. He turned to me. "We were on our way to see you, actually, Tam – is now a good time?"

"Sure boys – come on through."

They followed me like I was leading them to the slaughter. I wondered what the hell they were so worried about.

116

Inspector Bill Wyckham
LB 81

"White collar crims, eh? That's a turn up for the books. In Lothing, they think 'white collar crime' means nicking a fancy shirt from Albany's." I chuckled to myself as I pictured the top-tier gentlemen's formal wear shop, round the corner from a chippy, a pet shop, and the Romany-run pawnbrokers. Most of the coppers in the area were convinced Albany's had to be a front – couldn't see how there was the legitimate business in Lothing, given what ninety percent of the blokes in the town looked like on any given day, but, so far, no one had found anything to indicate that Albany's was anything other than a somewhat old-fashioned, modestly successful retail concern. They weren't setting any fires in the retail world, and neither staff nor owners would become millionaires anytime soon, but they were ticking over, somehow. Weddings, funerals, and high school proms obviously paid just enough, just often enough, to keep them hanging on.

Tam Freud laughed along with me. "Too right." She paused. "There's...an added complication, though."

I sighed. "When is there ever not? What is it this time?"

"Tony Raglan."

I groaned. "Hell's bells. What's he done now?"

"Maybe nothing...probably nothing. It's just... Max Rockford is a person of interest in the inquiry."

"And Tony Raglan's ex. Who came to you with this?" It'd bloody well better've been Tony Raglan. If it was anyone else, I'd hang Raglan out to dry. He knew the way the land lay, these days.

"He did, Sir. Tony, I mean."

"Good."

I deliberately didn't ask if she thought Feroc Hanson had convinced him to do the right thing. I preferred to soothe myself with at least the semblance of the belief that my officers were conscientious about playing by the rules. I looked at Tam Freud.

"Do you think their relationship is going to be an issue?"

"No, Sir. Tony's always put the uniform before anything else. I think he'd even put it before Feroc, if push came to shove."

"I wouldn't bank on that. What does Feroc think?"

"Feroc?"

"He's the best judge of Tony Raglan I've ever met, and I include myself in that assessment."

"I haven't asked him."

"I will. And then I'll let you know whether Raglan can be involved in this or not."

"We're going on record, though? About Rockford?"

"Yes. This is by the book – it can't be any other way. Not with a new Superintendent yet to be broken in."

"Do you think he's going to be okay?"

"Oh, he'll settle down. The always do. Six months of righteousness, and then it's back to standard operating procedure. Could you send Feroc Hanson through here? Find something for Tony to do, keep him busy for half an hour. Maybe remind him he needs to write up his IRBs."

"I thought incident reports were supposed to be contemporaneous?"

"I consider it contemporaneous with Tony Raglan if the report hits my desk in the same shift set as his notes were taken. I just backdate my signature."

"How do you square that with a computerised entry?"

I tapped the side of my nose. "That's a little trick you'll be taught when you get your stripes, D.C. Freud." I smiled, a little sadly. "Anyway, Tony's been a lot better with getting his paperwork sorted since the shooting – he still isn't completely convinced Feroc won't be transferred, so he's trying to behave himself."

 "What's he going to do when Feroc gets promoted? I mean, the kid's clearly bright – he's not going to be a plod for ever."

I looked at Tam Freud. "Do you not think Tony's intelligent, then? Academic smarts aren't the only kind of intelligence, you know?"

She blushed. "I didn't mean it like that, Sir -"

"No. I don't think you know *what* you mean, do you? You're wrong about Tony, you know."

She went quiet, and then said, softly: "I'll go and find Feroc, Sir."

"You do that. And, while you're keeping Tony Raglan out of the way, think about what I've just said to you. Think about everything you know about him. Think about your attitude, and the things he's been through."

I watched her leave, and felt an unreasoning anger course through me. I'd always had a bit of a soft spot for Tony Raglan. He wasn't intelligent in the traditional, obvious sense, but he knew what he was about. He could read situations better than any copper I'd met. He was clever when it came to people, which couldn't always be said about the academic types. He had brains – they just resulted in him thinking in a different way. Perhaps even seeing in a different way. He was often out of line, true, but being out of line often meant he kicked over a stone that the line would have walked clear past, sending all the interesting, important bits of darkness scurrying, screaming, into the light.

My wife, Charlotte, often talked about 'artists' eyes', the way creative people saw things that, to other people, weren't there until they were pointed out. My mother talked about 'the Sight', always crossing herself as she did so, and glancing nervously about, as though making sure there were no lurking mages in her living room.

I didn't know what gift or curse Tony Raglan had, but it made him one of the best coppers I'd had the pleasure of working with. It made him a man everyone wanted watching their back.

And it gave him a quiet confidence that was rarely shaken. Tony Raglan was bombproof – or he had been, until last year.

Last year had shaken him, but something like last year would have destroyed other coppers. We'd all been shaken by the shooting, especially those of us who'd seen the big, powerful Tony Raglan curled up on his side, pale and bleeding, moaning in agony, his eyes, which were always focused either on the person he was talking to, or at a point in the distance, eyes which were always taking in everything and everyone around him, closed against the horror, pain, and fear.

Last year, Tony Raglan had been afraid, and that had frightened all of us.

Not for the first time, since I'd come to Lothing as a newly-minted Sergeant, did I find myself wondering about Tony Raglan, wondering what really made him tick. Why he seemed so unable to hold his moments of brilliance. How he could have you swearing you'd give your life for him one moment, and screaming that you were going to murder him the next.

He was a contradiction, but it was more than that. Most human beings are contradictions – it's what makes us complete, whole, and functional individuals -but Tony Raglan had something beyond basic contradiction. He was more than mere complexity.

It wasn't mere complexity that gave that strange sense of lupine energy I got from him. It wasn't mere complexity that had seen him serve a quarter of a century in a role that often caused burnout within three years, if the individual in question failed to achieve promotion in that time. It wasn't mere complexity that meant that, by his own admission, Tony Raglan had no intention of seeking promotion. He was happy where he was, doing what he did. It annoyed the hell out of senior officers, who had reports to file that centred around 'maximisation of resource potential' and 'manifestation of appropriate career trajectory', and which saw a man who was a damn good street copper wanting to remain a street copper as a failure. But the people of Lothing seemed to value Tony Raglan's constancy, and I could see why.

Lothing was not only a coastal town, a place on the edge – it was a border town. And edges and borders are difficult places in which to live. They exist in a state of permanent impermanence, and this is reflected in the lives and natures of their settled populations, manifesting as a restlessness, an agitation, and a propensity of disorder, of both the private and public kind.

Tony Raglan's seemingly eternal presence was a kind of anti-venom for the worse excesses of Lothing's discordant energy fields. People liked seeing him, liked knowing they would continue seeing him. I'd seen him diffuse a riot looking for a spark to set it off simply by getting out of the Area Car, and asking one of the ring leaders why he was wasting a nice day being a muppet.

Those had been his exact words - "Stuart! Stuart Gregory! What d'you want to waste a day like today being a muppet for, eh? The cells aren't airconditioned, you know, and we don't offer cold beer in the evening."

The fledging riot had peered around, flapped its tiny wings a couple of times, chirped amongst itself for a bit – and then decided to eat out of Tony Raglan's hand. And Stuart Gregory wasn't a casual criminal – he was a career Punk. If there was any kind of action against the status quo and the ruling elite, Stuart Gregory would be there. If politicians and business leaders were getting nasty surprises in their mail, Stuart Gregory would probably be involved in the sending of said nasty surprises. Animal rights, Black Lives Matter, AntiFa – if it required a show of force to make a point, Stuart Gregory was there.

And yet he wasn't an unpleasant bloke, when it came down to it. He was well-read, intelligent, and drank knowledge the way most of my relief drank lager. He was a vegetarian, and had explained exactly why that lifestyle was more sustainable, environmentally, and more socially sound, than veganism. He'd made a lot of sense, talking about use of land, freight miles and associated carbon footprints, and ableism in dietary fads. He and Tony would often end up having long, involved chats whenever Gregory got pulled in. It was an unlikely friendship – as unlikely as Tony's friendship with Steven Lassiter.

I paused, feeling a flash of regret as I thought about Lassiter. He shouldn't have died. There was no reason for him to have killed himself. It'd only made things worse for Tony, on top of the woman dying in the crash.

That was another thing about Tony Raglan: people were quick to judge him as an insensitive bastard, and yet he often felt things far more deeply than other people. They stayed with him, haunted him.

I'd known him long enough to know he suffered more than most people knew, and more than he'd ever admit. I wanted to ease that suffering for him, but didn't have the first clue how.

P.C. Tony Raglan
LB 265

"Tam – back so soon?"

"Just can't get enough of you, Tony. Although, this time, it's Feroc I want. Or, rather, Inspector Wyckham wants him. He asked me to remind you about writing up your IRBs."

I pulled a face. "I hate writing. Makes my arm ache."

"You should work out more. Lift weights. Press ups. It's poor muscle condition, that's all."

"You've not heard of repetitive strain injury, then?"

Tam Freud smiled. "Surely, to get repetitive strain injury, you'd have to be *repetitively* writing? As in, on a regular basis?"

"I do my IRBs every day. That's repetitive."

"Not the only thing. Where's Feroc?"

"Needed to pee. He should be back in a sec."

"I'll wait."

"What does Wyckham want?"

"He wants Feroc. On his own."

I stared at Freud. "It's about Max, then."

"Yeah."

"Look, I'm not a complete prat. I'm not going to bulldoze in there. And, if I can't be part of this job, I can't. I'm okay with that. I want a conviction here, Tam, and if I need to stay out of the way so we can get one, then I'm gone. Way, way gone. Alright? You're not dealing with a probationer here. Or some lovesick swain."

She raised her hands. "Woah. Who said anything like that? I know you're cool with how things have to play out."

"Do you?"

"Yes. Of course I do. You're an experienced copper. Everyone knows how much the Job means to you. You wouldn't do anything to screw it up."

I sat down, arms folded across my chest, head down. "But I did. Last year. Remember?"

I saw the memories flash across her eyes. I didn't know if she'd got to the pub while I was still down, bleeding out on the tiled floor, or whether I was already on my way to hospital by that point. But even if she hadn't seen me, she would have seen the photos in the papers, photos taken on smartphones, horror fighting with a desire to record part of a person's history. Like every copper, I hated the amateur snappers that got all over everything like a rash, or a bad aftershave, but, unlike other coppers, I understood them. People felt adrift in the modern world, as though they weren't really real. Technology had taken over so much of our lives that, for a lot of people, it had pushed them to the fringes of their own existence. It was natural that people who felt marginalised wanted to prove that they existed. That they experienced things. That they *were.* And, in the 21st century, those needs were met by creating photographic records, just as in Neolithic times the prototypes of us would have recorded their existence in scratches on stone. Just as we've previously recorded our existence in paintings, books, music, and poetry. The only reason we sneer at the modern habit of whipping out a smartphone to record passing existence is because that form of history keeping is open to everyone. Even the working classes.

Britain has never been comfortable with the idea of the working classes recording their own history – their words might contradict the established, Establishment narrative.

The door opened, and Feroc stepped into the room, pausing when he saw Tam Freud. I raised an eyebrow. "Wyckham wants you."

"Oh?"

"Yeah. Private conversation. I've been reminded that I have IRBs to write up." I rubbed my wrist, pulling a face of exaggerated pain.

"You'll live." Feroc grinned at me, then turned to Tam. "Now?"

She nodded. "Now."

"Catch you later, Tone."

"Yeah. Cash me ousside, yeah?"

Feroc and Tam, catching the cultural reference, both laughed.

Feroc shook his head. "I don't think people are going to be conned out of a million or whatever that dozy cow got again."

"She's hardly a dozy cow if she can get that kind of money for no effort, is she?" Tam commented. I shrugged.

"In my experience, D.C. Freud, the people who get paid the most typically put in the least effort. It's why the D.C. Comics brigade upstairs get paid more than those of us who risk life and limb on a daily basis."

"Oh, hush. You have your bright, shiny new stab vests, don't you?"

"Won't stop a bullet. Especially not if you take it off duty."

The room fell silent. I'd been surprised by the bitterness in my own voice: I'd thought I was over the shooting. It was more than a year ago, after all. I'd always prided myself on moving on from things quickly. What the hell was happening to me?"

"Sometimes it doesn't even stop a blade. That guy in London." Feroc's voice was strained. I nodded, and met his eyes, trying to give him some of my own strength. The Force couldn't lose a copper like Feroc. I didn't doubt he'd make Superintendent, one day – if the despair that dogs us all didn't drag him under first.

"You'd best run along and have your little chat with Wyckham." I grinned. "Don't worry about me, I'm sure I won't die here, all alone, clutching my pen in a rictus of agony."

"No one ever died from writing."

"Bob Marley died jogging."

"Oh, so that's your excuse, is it?"

"It's not an excuse. Not doing something because someone actually *died* doing the thing is a *reason*. And don't start with driving – driving is unavoidable."

"I don't think it is – there are people who don't drive. Who can't drive."

"Yeah, and ask them how easy and fulfilling their day to day lives are."

"You're just bigoted."

"No, I just like cars. And driving."

"Yeah, and people who support the renewal of Trident just like submarines."

"Maybe some of them do."

"Well, I can't think of any other reason for renewing it."

"How about, we haven't been the target of a nuclear attack since we've had Trident?"

"Maybe that just means no one rates us enough to go to the trouble and expense of nuking us. But sure, we can just blow up Scotland if we ever did need to launch Trident."

"I don't see a problem with that. Other than whiskey, what've those miserable gits ever given us?"

"Oh, I don't know... Most of our culture...Half of our land, or more...A significant proportion of our language..." I caught Tam Freud, trying to cover her laughter, as Feroc regarded me with the look of a precocious child who's just outwitted a grown up in a test of logic.

I shook my head. "See? Writing disagrees with me."

Feroc sighed. "D'you want me to write up your IRB for you, once I'm done with Wyckham?" He glanced at Tam Freud. "You didn't hear that, by the way."

"Hear what? I've got terrible tinnitus, came on really suddenly."

"Good girl."

I shook my head. "No. Better not. Besides, doing something I don't like'll be good practice for other, more enduring things I'd rather not do. Retiring from the Job. Dying."

"Stars and stones, Tony, that's morbid – you're nowhere near either of those things yet, man!"

"Nearer than you. And last year was a close call with the latter."

Feroc shook his head. "If you're done with your Emo reverie, I'd better go and talk to Wyckham. Why don't you put some Bullet for my Valentine on, give you something suitable to work to?"

"Screw you."

"Not at work – it takes too long to get the uniform off."

I was laughing out loud as the door swung shut behind Tam and Feroc. I couldn't stay lost in my thoughts for long with Feroc around – he seemed to instinctively know how to pull me out of myself, get me back on track.

I wondered how I'd feel when he inevitably got promotion, which would almost certainly involve a transfer. Lothing had had its share of coppers staying on after winning promotion. Of course, all being well, we'd still be sharing a home together, but I wondered about how it would feel, to go back to not working with him.

He hadn't been at Lothing all that long – he wasn't even two years out of probation, yet – and yet I couldn't remember what it had been like before he'd turned up, and we'd started working together. Just as I couldn't remember what it had been like before the shooting last year, before we were finally honest with each other, and became Lothing's most famous couple. To my way of thinking, the fact that I couldn't remember those things meant they would never come to pass again, would never be relevant again. I hoped my way of thinking was accurate.

With a sigh, I picked up my notebook, flicked through it, then hunched forward, focusing on the formal record sheet on the table in front of me. My wrist was aching already.

D.I. Mark Roscoe

"So, what do we reckon is going on with this Clifford-Alistair?" I regarded Tam Freud, tapping the top of my pen against the edge of my desk. It didn't mean anything: I used to get in trouble for it at high school, many years ago now. A psychiatrist would probably spin some story about how I was uncertain in my masculinity, and the pen represented a phallus, and the tapping against wood related to a sense of redundancy, blah, blah, blah. It was just a habit, probably arising from the fact that I didn't like silence. No mystery, no deep symbolism, no ramifications for my identity. A simple habit. Nothing more.

"Not sure, guv, but there's definitely something off about him. He's too charming – or what he thinks is charming. Plus, most people with the intelligence to set up investments know that they're not guaranteed, and they're certainly not stable. Especially not when you're dealing with relatively young funds, which those Eastern Rise manage are. I mean, Eastern Rise themselves are a young company, in industry terms – they've only been going five years."

"That sounds dodgy all by itself, surely?"

Tam shook her head. "Not necessarily. Everyone has to start somewhere. What it does flag up is that they may well be mainly dealing with virgin investors, who are at greater risk of being ripped off, if that is what's going on."

Feroc Hanson looked up, frowning. "What's puzzling me is, I can't see how Clifford-Alistair can be doing this on his own. Someone else at the firm has got to be in on it."

Tam turned to him. "The only other person listed as having any kind of relationship with Eastern Rise Investments is some species of "consultant", Andrew Parker-James. He's got a long rap with the Financial Conduct Authority, but nothing bad enough to get him struck off. Mind you, the FCA pretty much only kick guys like Parker-James to the kerb once we've already binned them, and they don't really have a choice about acting."

It was my turn to frown. "He must have staff, though?"

"Not that we can find on record, guv."

"What about off the record?"

"I don't even know how we'd begin with that. I mean, sure, we can turn up during working hours, see who's about, but all he has to say is anyone there is an intern, the jobcentre sent them for work experience, he's giving them a bit of work experience as a favour to their dad, who's a mate, they're a mate that he's helping get back on their feet..."

Feroc shook his head, a hint of anger in the gesture. "Someone should tell the DWP that this habit they have of shunting people off for unpaid work experience is making it a bugger to keep tabs on the illegal employment racket."

I raised an eyebrow. "Oh, they know that. They just don't care. Why do you think you have an easier time getting the wrinkles out of a Shar Pei's face than info out of that bunch of wa – jokers?"

Feroc started laughing. "What? What's so funny? C'mon – share the joke."

"It's just Tony's nickname for the DWP, guv – Deadbeat Wankers and Prats."

Tony Raglan, lounging against the far wall, smirked. bI laughed. "Sounds about right. Anyway, all I've been able to call up on Clifford-Alistair is a previous, twenty-odd years ago, for possession. A bit of waccy-baccy." Tam and Feroc both shared a look and a smile. "What? Do we not say 'waccy-baccy' any more?"

Tam shook her head. "Not really, guv. It's blow, grass, hash -"

"I thought hash was heroin."

Feroc shook his head, echoing Tam's earlier gesture. "No, guv. Heroin is H, or Horse."

"I thought ketamine was horse?"

"No, guv. You give ketamine to horses, but its street name is Special K."

Tony Raglan grinned. "Well, that'd improve the breakfast cereal."

Feroc turned to him, rolling his eyes. "Like you've ever eaten Special K."

"Children," I stood up as a ball of scrap paper, thrown by Tony at Feroc, sailed across the room. I caught it in midair, and glared around the room until everyone managed to get a grip of themselves.

"So, other than a little bit of personal naughtiness when he was young and daft, we've got nothing on Clifford-Alistair. Apart from an interesting little scent of suspicion that never went anywhere." Everyone's ears pricked up. "I thought that'd get your attention. Yes, he was a person of interest, but, it would seem, either clean, or Teflon. Nothing stuck to him."

"What was the suspicion, guv?"

"Art fraud."

I noticed Tony Raglan pale. I frowned, wondering what his problem was, and continued. "Anyway, nothing stuck, so we can't bring that previous into anything. CPS don't even like us bringing *actual* previous into things, never mind circumstantial and suspicion. Tony? You alright? Got something to add?"

"It might be nothing, guv, but there's a bloke I know...Max Rockford. He's in the art business, and...well, he took a kicking recently, but he's not being straight about how it happened."

"You think he's working with Clifford-Alistair?"

"I don't know, guv, but Clifford-Alistair would need someone on the sharp end of the art side of things if he's up to his old tricks. What was the suspicion, last time?"

"There was a rumour going round that he was commissioning good quality fakes, but charging his clients for the real deal. Something your boy would be in on?"

"Maybe." Tony seemed awkward, and I watched Feroc and Tam watching him. They clearly knew more about Tony and this Max character than I did. "I mean...he wouldn't see it as a crime. Max, I mean. He'd deliberately do things so that any expert would spot that it wasn't kosher straight off. He's honest like that. Well, honest after a fashion, I suppose. I know he's done close copies for people who knew they were buying a fake, but couldn't hope to afford the real thing. Max's work's good – it meant something to these people that Max Rockford'd painted it. It's why they didn't just go and buy a poster from some gallery giftshop."

"And if he's moved in to something more sophisticated? Clifford-Alistair, I mean. Would this Max play along with him?"

"I don't know, guv. I think he might, if Clifford-Alistair spun him a story about how the scheme meant artists were hitting back at the Establishment. If he told him it was about new talent getting known *and* getting paid. Max cares about stuff like that."

A light clicked on. "And you care about Max?"

Tony shook his head, resolutely. "Not enough to scupper this, guv. If he's involved, he goes down."

"Good man. That's the kind of attitude I like to see. Feroc, just remember – never cross this guy, right? He'll slit your throat, feed you to the wolves, and probably use your blood for eyeliner."

There was a ripple of laughter. I let it happen.

"Now," I waited as the silence fell. "There's one scheme in particular that seems to be a little jumpy – something called 'Avin' an Art Attack. Tony, can you call up the Eastern Rise website?"

Tony turned to the laptop beside him, and began tapping keys. He suddenly went still. "Tony?"

"It's on the main page, guv. And reading through it, it's exactly the sort of thing Max Rockford could be talked into getting mixed up with."

"Print it out, please. A copy for everyone."

"Guv."

"Tam – what's the law on misleading investors?" She shook her head. "Pretty much non-existent, guv, unless it's really blatant. Pretty much, as long as you use clear English, and people are given at least 7 days to change their mind – 14 is considered best practice – once they've signed, it's legal."

"That's madness! So, you're ripping someone off, but, because they consented to it, ripping them off becomes okay?"

"Pretty much, guv. It's the idea that people are reasonable, competent adults – unless there's no chance in hell they could have understood what they were getting in to, it's assumed they did understand, and were happy about it."

"Jesus. You'll be saying people can consent to being raped and having seven bells beaten out of them, as long as it's explained prettily, and they sign on the dotted line, next."

Tony grinned. "Well, that is already sort of a thing, guv."

"What?"

"BDSM."

"Don't get me started on that shite. You can't consent to abuse. End of."

"I don't know, guv." I stared at Tam. She continued, "I've got a mate – not in the Job – she's into that scene. I went along with her to a … well, a sort of house party, I suppose. It wasn't too bad, actually. No one came on to me, everyone was completely appropriate. I felt safer there than I do on a Friday or Saturday night down the Heart of -" Her hand flew to her mouth, and she turned to face Tony Raglan. "Sorry! I didn't think!"

He shrugged. "It's okay. I'm not going to fall to pieces, start sobbing about being triggered, demand a safe space. I got shot. I'm still here. The guy who pulled the trigger's inside, and won't be out for a bloody long time. Nothing to get upset about."

"Just as well, really. " Feroc's eyes gleamed with friendly malice. "I don't think they do safe spaces in your size – the social justice brigade tend to be somewhat elfin and fragile."

"Probably all that veganism."

I closed my eyes, relaxing into the laughter and banter. How long would this last, I wondered, once we only had coppers with degrees? And once we lost this, how long before that steel bright edge that saw men like Tony Raglan through things like getting gut shot, was also lost? How long, after the degrees, until the robots?

I opened my eyes. "Alright, you lot. Simmer down. Tam – I know you've got a statement from the Ravenswood woman, but I want you to talk to everyone who was involved in the disturbance outside Eastern Rise's offices. Get statements from all of them. Take Gerry and Micha with you, that'll get it done quicker."

"Guv." The three of them headed out of the office, grabbing coats, voices rising and falling. I turned to Feroc. "Do you know this guy, Max?"

"A little, guv. I mean, I've met him. Professionally, and briefly off duty. He came to visit Tony in the hospital, last year."

"But you don't know him beyond that?"

"No, guv."

"Good. Go and talk to him. See what he has to say about all this. He's not under arrest, unless that becomes unavoidable – he's helping us with enquiries, right?"

"Guv."

"Tony – you're with me. Your Inspector says you need to become better friends with paperwork."

"Guv."

"You understand this isn't personal?" I watched Feroc Hanson leave. "I just can't give anyone any reason to light a fire up my arse on this."

"I understand, guv. It's okay – I wouldn't feel right questioning Max, anyway."

"How do you know him, out of curiosity?"

Tony smiled, a distant ghost of memories. "He used to have Feroc's place, guv."

"Ah. And, his, ah, extra curricular activities?"

Tony shook his head. "If there was anything, he kept it from me, guv."

"Yes. I suppose he would've done. I want you to know, Tony, I hope we're wrong about this."

"I don't. I didn't like Clifford-Alistair from the off."

"That's interesting." Tony Raglan had sound instincts. If he didn't take to someone, there was usually a good reason. "Why was that?"

"I don't know. I mean, he's a smarmy git, and prejudiced as all hell, but that's nothing new."

"Prejudiced against you?"

"Me, Aimee Gardner, Tam Freud, the police in general."

"Oh. One of those."

"And then some. No, he was a smarmy git, but it was more than that. He felt wrong. Not dangerous, but like he'd enjoy getting one over on you."

"So this sounds like him, then?"

"Oh, definitely."

"Okay. Well, we'll just have to see what turns up."

"Guv."

"Anyway – while we're waiting, let me give you a very brief introduction to the world of art crime, what little I know of it from what few books and resources I have to hand."

"Guv."

I stood up, and beckoned to Tony to follow me. Halfway to the door, I turned.

"About last year – were you on the level when you said it didn't bother you? Tam Freud mentioning the pub, I mean?"

"Honestly?"

"Please."

"I'm bloody terrified of the place. Haven't been in there since. I won't even walk by it if I can help it. When I hear drunks shouting in the street outside mine, I still wake up in a cold sweat. I'm jumpy as a cat on a hot tin roof in pubs generally. I have to sit where no one can get behind me, and where I can see the door. I won't go up to the bar to order – someone else always has to. I tried once, a few weeks ago – started shaking and feeling dizzy. Feroc had to get me home." He took a deep, rasping breath, bowed his head, and looked away.

My heart broke for him, Tony Raglan was the copper all the lads wanted to be, the driver all my guys wanted on their team for a raid. He was the one everyone looked to for protection, the one we all trusted to have our backs. The thought of him being afraid, waking up in a sweat, having panic attacks, made me feel a blinding rage towards Matthew Youngman, and everyone like him.

Tony Raglan had become human in my eyes, and in that becoming, he'd killed a part of himself.

Or perhaps that part of him had already been dead. Perhaps a version of Tony Raglan did die that night, bleeding out on the floor of the Heart of Darkness, spilled blood mingling with spilled beer, heartbeats fading to the shadows of the footsteps gone

before. I looked him right in the eye. "You're safe now. Always."
He nodded. "Guv."
We stood in silence. Not an awkward silence, but the kind of
silence human beings fall into when we run out of language. That
happens a lot when your language is English, I've found: English
has a lot of things that it doesn't allow to exist in words. Finally, I
shook off the spell, and found the words my language allowed.
  "Right – that's enough moping. Time to get to work." I paused.
"I'm assuming you *can* read? I mean, I've never thought to ask
before -"
Tony grinned. "I'm alright until we get to the big words, guv. I
have to sound them out, out loud."
"I can live with that. It's art – it'll probably be mostly pictures,
anyway."

P.C. Feroc Hanson
LB 599

Max looked as though he was going somewhere when I pulled up at the Marina. He was stepping off the gangplank, wearing a beaten-up leather jacket. He saw me, and I saw the thought of running cross his face.

I shook my head. "I'm not Tony Raglan – I can run faster than you."

"You reckon?"

"I know. Because I didn't take a kicking a few days ago because I lost my bottle after I robbed one old lady, but the money I nicked off her wasn't enough for the people I needed to pay back."

"I didn't give them the money. I couldn't, not in the end. That's what the kicking was for. If I'd handed it over, it would've been alright. They'd've given me time to get the rest. But I told them I didn't have it." ⸱

"But you did. You'd stolen it from Angela Dalloway."

"Who?"

"Eighty-seven Beresford Avenue?"

"Oh. I never knew who lived there. It's alright, though – I mean, I gave the money back. Well, I put it through the door. In an envelope. She wasn't there. I did knock."

Roscoe had said not to arrest Max unless I had to – he was helping with enquiries, for the moment. That's what Roscoe had said. And Tony would hate me. But it wasn't like I'd *planned* on getting a confession. They weren't meant to roll over and die so easily.

"She's gone to stay with her brother. She left a message at the station, in case we needed to speak to her again."

"Oh. D'you think the money'll be alright?"

"It will if scroats like you don't go breaking in. What made you choose that house, anyway?"

"It was all so stupid... I'd been at a mate's. I was in the shop, and heard her going on about the money she kept in a biscuit tin, how she was saving up for a coach holiday, or something. I followed her back, noticed which house she lived in. Then I parked my car on the street, and kept an eye during the daytime until she went to the shop again. I hadn't thought she'd be so daft as to leave the key in the back door."

"She won't be again. She lets her cat out that way."

"Oh."

"You took the skull, and the gin, too, didn't you?"

He nodded. "I couldn't get the skull back through the letter box. And I'd drunk half the gin. I did put an extra twenty in with the money, so she can buy another bottle."

"Have you still got the skull?"

"Yes."

"Give it here." I shook out an evidence bag. "I'll keep it for her until she gets back."

Max rummaged in a pocket of the jacket, and pulled the skull out. "I don't know why I took that, really. Impulse, I suppose."

"Like the tarot cards?"

He shook his head violently. "No way. I wouldn't steal tools. Not that kind, anyway. They wouldn't have worked for me, not being stolen."

He had Tony's attitude to magical items, then: that you had to come by them honestly, either through choosing them, or being given them. Otherwise, they were nothing more than toys. Crafting them was the absolute best way you could get them – I'd watched Tony carving his rune set. Had watched him collect pebbles from the beach, and spend an entire afternoon patiently chiselling the symbols into the stone. Then the following morning painting the cuts in with gold paint and a fine brush. Then varnishing the stones, to seal the paintwork, and placing them by the waterfeature in the back yard to set. I remembered questioning the wisdom of placing them near water – surely it would mean the varnish took longer to set? What if the stones got wet? What if it rained?

Tony had simply smiled. "It doesn't matter. Stones need to be charged by water, because only water can destroy them."

I hadn't understood, and had said so. Tony had nodded. "Of course you don't. No one's taught you, have they?"

I hadn't realised Heathenry *was* taught, beyond the self-teaching of reading around it, and encountering and encouraging the views of other Heathens.

"Of course it's taught. That's what elders are for. But you're right, it starts with enjoyment, with feelings, with personal exploration. But you've had that time, I think. Soon, I'll have to start your education. Which will culminate in you creating your own rune set."

Personally, I wasn't in a rush to get to that point – I couldn't imagine ever understanding the symbols. But Tony had carved his runes while he was recovering from being shot, and it had taken pretty much all the magical energy he had. I'd seen him fade, once the runes were done. It was as though he'd poured himself, his soul, into them, and now had to wait for those things to be returned to him. In the meantime, he'd passed on to me the runes he'd been using up until he'd carved his own, a beautiful set, the runes painted silver on onyx gemstones, cocooned in a bag of burgundy velvet.

"They're not toys, of course, but you can play with them. Do that. Play with them. Make friends with them. Learn their voice, and their language."

Tony had held the bag of runes in both hands for a moment, his eyes closed. "What was chosen, is now given. Lessons learned are passed on, to be learned anew." Then, as gently as if he were handling a newborn kitten, he'd passed the bag to me.

Instinctively, I'd taken it with both hands, the way it had been handed to me.

"Play with them. And, when you're ready, come to me, and I'll teach you the formal meanings."

I returned my focus to Max. "But you did look at them?"

"Of course. I always like to see what tools other people use. Tony's the same, you probably will be, one day. Tony does it with cars, too. And guns." Max paused. "Well, he used to do it with guns. I don't know whether he's still into them the way he was...before."

I shook my head. "I haven't seen him with anything to do with guns."

"He had an armoury, in the spare room?"

"I use that for my writing. I've not seen any guns there."

"He's sold them, then. Or, knowing him, destroyed them. That's a shame."

"Is it?"

"Yes. They're just a tool, Feroc. Guns don't kill people. People kill people. It wasn't a gun that shot Tony last year – it was an angry, confused young man who'd made some bad choices."

"You sound like a social worker."

Max shrugged, and winced as though the movement pained him. "I've met more than my fair share of those."

"Oh yeah?"

"Yeah." That single word made it clear the subject was closed. I wasn't bothered by that – I had my own subject to pursue, and this was just a distraction.

"Who gave you the kicking?" *No suggestions. No leading questions. No words placed into mouths.*

"Guy called Andrew Parker-James. To be fair, he didn't look like he had it in him. Vicious little shit, though."

"And what did he want the money for? The money you stole from Mrs. Dalloway, but later returned?"

Max sighed.

"That's a long story, and, I think, one better told at your fine police station." He glanced at his watch. "Alexander will just have to stew, until he realises I'm not coming."

"Alexander Clifford-Alistair is in custody."

Max looked surprised. "Oh? Well, then, you really *do* need to hear my story in a formal setting."

I looked at him. He looked back. I fingered my cuffs, then picked up my radio.

"Lima-Bravo from five-nine-nine, receiving?"

"Go ahead, five-nine-nine."

"I need transport for one, down at Haven Marina. And not two-six-five. Repeat, do not send P.C. Raglan. Over."

There was a pause. "Received and understood. Stand by."

Alexander

I had planned to remain standing in the cell. It offered a sense of dignity, of being in control. It was a way of defying the petty attempts of these monkeys in uniforms to humiliate me, to make me small enough for them to handle.

But the few minutes I'd assumed I'd be waiting turned into half an hour. That became an hour. Then longer. I had to yield, in the end. Had to sit down on the high school gymnasium crash mat thrown on top of a wooden, built-in bench. A folded blanket of coarse grey wool implied this was supposed to serve as a bed, were I to be kept here overnight. I didn't imagine that would be the case.

I must have been in the cell for at least two hours – there was a window, barred, coated in the kind of glass one typically observed on the bases of old-fashioned milk bottles, and set too high in the wall for anyone to reach. It did let in light, and the shifting shades and shadows of a world that was carrrying on without me told me a significant amount of time had passed.

I couldn't understand why they'd taken my watch.

The sound was faint, at first, but drew closer: footsteps, a heavy, regular rhythm, and the jangle of metal. Keys, I thought, recognising the sound. Someone was walking towards the cells with a bunch of keys. Clearly, I was going to be released. I stood up as I heard a door slam closed. The footsteps, the keys, came deafeningly close, then stopped.

There was a grating of metal. The hatch in the centre of the cell door opened.

"Clifford-Alistair – face the wall, hands against the wall. Keep your head down."

I complied, feeling somewhat foolish, and the door swung open. "Walk towards me. Keep your hands where I can see them. Turn around, hands behind your back."

I braced myself for the harsh feel of metal, but it didn't come. Instead, one of my arms was gripped, firmly, and a uniformed officer stepped close to my side. "Move. Forward."

The cell door wasn't closed behind me. "My shoes?"

"You won't need them. Come on – walk."

"I want a solicitor." If the police were willing to ignore the health and safety protocols which recommended that footwear be worn on tiled surfaces, heaven only knows what games they'd play in an interview.

"Thought you said you didn't need one. Thought you were innocent."

"I am, but since you seem manifestly unconcerned as to whether I break my neck, or catch god knows what from walking near enough barefoot – these socks are pure silk, I'll have you know, and I do intend to bill you for any damage incurred to them – on this floor, I feel that legal representation might not, after all, be such a bad idea."

The officer grinned. I imagined wolves and sharks looked much the same when they bared their teeth.

"You'll have to go back into the cell and wait. This isn't a doctor's surgery – can't have people sitting around making the place look untidy."

"I have no intention of returning to the cells. I wish to have my solicitor called, and I shall wait in the front office, like a civilised member of decent society, until he arrives. Do I make myself clear?"

"Unfortunately, it's not up to you what happens, pal. This is our turf, now. Our rules. And, if you want your brief, you go back in the cell to wait for him."

"Jon – what's going on?"

"He says he wants a brief."

"I was told I had the right to request one at any time."

"DI Roscoe's waiting for him, yes?"

"Yeah."

The black sergeant shook her head. "If he wants a solicitor, Roscoe'll have to wait until they get here." She glanced up at me. "Do you have a solicitor you'd like us to contact?"

"Yes. His card's in the wallet you took from me earlier. David Marchant. He's based in London."

The sergeant exchanged a look with the officer holding me.

"Doubt he'll make it here inside of a couple of hours. And that's with little traffic, imagining he's able to leave right away, and we can even get hold of him."

"The third number on the card is his home number," I interrupted, beginning to feel slightly panicky.

The sergeant shook her head. "Put him back. I'll call his brief, tell Roscoe to schedule the interview for first thing. You know his brief's going to insist he can't possibly be interviewed at this late hour, when he gets here."

"True."

"Look, I don't see how you have grounds to keep me here. Bail me, I'll come in in the morning, with my solicitor."

The sergeant glared at me. "You don't get to make requests here, you know. And no way am I bailing you. You have money, a car, you know someone with a boat moored literally across the road from your office -"

"Do I? I don't think I mentioned that."

"You didn't. But he did. He seemed to know you rather better than he would care to, to be honest. Certainly better than is sensible. So, you're not being bailed. Take him back to the cells. He can have his dinner while I call his brief. See what he has to say."

"Shall I give the Regency a bell, see if they've got rooms?"

"Not a bad idea. That way Mr. Clifford-Alistair can speak to his solicitor tonight, prior to his formal interview, as PACE recommends."

"You might want to take the Police and Criminal Evidence Act a little more seriously, you know."

"And you, pal, might want to shut up. Before you slip in those nice silk socks of yours, and crack your head on something. Easily happen, on tiled flooring..."

"Jon." The sergeant's voice was a bored warning.

"Only riling him, Sarge."

"Well, just rile him right back into his box, okay? I'll let Roscoe know, and call his solicitor." Turning to me, she said: "It's sausage and mash for tea. You did specify no special dietary needs."

"I'm beginning to wish I hadn't. What's the vegetarian option?"

"Cheesy mash and beans. The vegan option is plain mashed potato."

"I'm underwhelmed."

"Can't have the taxpayer thinking scum are getting better grub than poor old dears in nursing homes, can we, now? Take him back, Jon, before he gets on my nerves."

"Come on. Back you go."

We reached the cell just as another officer was walking along the line of doors, shouting to occupants to stand away from the door, opening the hatch, and placing the kind of plastic tray primary school children are given on the ledge that sat just inside the hatch.

He looked up as we approached. "Room service for this one, too?"

"Yep. Just the usual. He decided he wanted a brief. Just as we were going in to interview."

"Typical. His is being kept warm in the kitchen – I'd thought he'd be out when I was doing my rounds."

"So did he – outside."

"More fool him then."

"What I told him."

"Excuse me – I am standing right here!"

"Not for long." I was pushed towards the open cell door. "In you go." The door slammed shut behind me.

"My solicitor -"

"Is being called. Will get here when he gets here."

"I want to see him straight away."

"Of course you do. And we will do our very best to facilitate that. Now, shut up, and sit down. There's a good boy."

I could understand the marks where a succession of inmates had clearly punched the wall.

"I will be making a formal complaint about this!"

"Of course you will. I'll drop the complaints form round with your dinner. I'm not authorised to give you a pen, so you'll have to wait until your brief gets here. He'll help you fill it in." The hatch slammed shut. It had been dark before. It was pitch black, now.

D.I. Mark Roscoe

"Right. Right. Yeah. Okay. Well, it'll have to be, won't it? What time's his brief getting here? No, I'll turn 'em loose. They can get some kip, we'll come at him fresh in the morning. Gives us a bit of an advantage, anyway, doesn't it."

I slammed the phone down, and tried hard to calm myself, rather than punching a wall.

"Guv?"

Tony Raglan looked up, a question in his dark eyes. "Something wrong?"

"Clifford-Alistair's called for a brief. We can't interview him until morning, now."

"What's brought that on?"

I sighed. "He probably suspects that we've spoken to Max Rockford, or that we will do. He can't trust Max to keep schtum, so he's getting jumpy and playing silly buggers. You may as well get off home. Get some kip."

"Is Feroc back yet?"

I shook my head. "I don't know. Go downstairs, find out. Then both of you, knock it on the head for tonight." I pulled my mobile out of my pocket. "I'll call Tam and the others, tell them to wrap up."

"We'll get him, guv."

"Oh, I know we will. We're always close once they ask for a brief. If Feroc's not back, have Aimee Gardner give him a shout. Tell him to bring Rockford in."

"Guv."

I watched Tony Raglan leave, feeling a rising wave of frustration. While this kind of hold up was a fairly common delaying tactic for people new to contact with the police to use, thinking it would get them released on bail at the very least, it always riled me. The best way to have things go smoothly for you if you were brought into police custody was to make any requests for legal representation, or to see a doctor or member of the clergy, at the outset, calmly and politely, and remain calm and polite throughout. If you were put in a cell, sit down on the bench, with your hands out in front of you, and don't make too much noise.

We call people who act like that "compliant prisoners", and we treat them with a little bit more courtesy. No strong arm tactics, and we'll remember to check in as to whether they want a drink of water every so often.

I hadn't wanted to have Clifford-Alistair here overnight. I'd planned to interview him, and either release him without charge, or formally charge him and ship him into the custody of the magistrates' court in Norwich. But it looked like he was going to be here, now, which was a bugger – it meant we couldn't hold him after the interview tomorrow. Hopefully, his brief would have the good sense to tell him to 'fess up. That would speed things along nicely, and he'd be off our hands.

That was going to be another issue: if things fell the way they seemed to be shaping up, the embezzlement charge would be void. I wasn't sure what we could charge him with – misrepresentation of some kind, potentially obtaining monies by deception? I groaned. This had all the hallmarks of something I'd have to pass on to the Financial Intelligence Unit, or the Financial Conduct Authority. As the FIU were part of our mob, I decided to call them first.

I picked up the phone on my desk, and scanned the Post-It note attached to the board behind it. Then I tapped in a number, and waited.

I was about to hang up, assuming nobody was about, when the phone was finally answered, by a voice and a name I recognised from time spent in Edinburgh ten years ago.

"Duncan! How the hell are you these days? It's Mark, Mark Roscoe. I'm out in Lothing now. Suffolk. On the coast. No, not one of the posh parts. All down and dirty here. I've got a bit of an odd one – out of the norm for us, and probably something we'll have to punt your way – mind if I run it by you? He's sobbing for a solicitor, so we won't be interviewing him until the morning, now – probably just as well, as it looks like the charge has already shifted. Yeah, like I said – tricky."

Sergeant Aimee Gardner
LB 761

I looked up as Feroc Hanson came in, accompanying the prisoner he should absolutely not have been even thinking of arresting.

"Feroc – what part of 'do not arrest Max Rockford' did you fail, spectacularly, to understand?"

"I couldn't help it, Sarge. He put his hand up to a burglary. What was I supposed to do?"

"Well, you weren't supposed to be questioning him about a burglary, for a start."

"I wasn't – he sort of assumed I knew, assumed that's why I was there -"

"Alright." I sighed, and beckoned Tony Raglan's ex up the desk. I had to confess, I was curious to actually see what this guy was about.

He wasn't bad looking. Younger than Tony, but older then Feroc, with a wildness to him – the kind of clean-cut bad-boy everyone finds irresistable.

"Full name?"

"Maximillian Rockford."

"Address?"

"Permanent address, or the local one?"

"You have two addresses, Mr. Rockford?"

"I've a flat in Norwich, and a boat at Haven Marina."

"If you could provide both, please." He did. "Date of birth?"

"January twenty-seventh, 1980."

Thirty-seven, then.

"Occupation?"

"Artist. Self-employed."

"Do you understand why you've been brought here this evening?"

"Yes. I stole money and property from a house in Beresford Avenue, a few days ago – sorry, I'm not good with dates and things like that. Days sort of blur into one another."

Feroc placed an evidence bag on the desk. I glanced at it, noting the crystal skull inside. "This is one of the items stolen from the property, Sarge. Mr. Rockford claims to have posted the money he stole back through the letterbox of number 87, Beresford Avenue, along with payment for a further item, a bottle of gin, which is, ah, no longer fully in his possession. He has expressed remorse over the burglary, but was operating under significant external pressure."

I raised an eyebrow. "And will he be telling us all about these external pressures?"

"Yes, Sarge."

"Good. Take him straight to interview, find out what he has to say for himself." I turned to Max. "As you've returned what property you are able from the burglary, and have admitted responsibility, you will be cautioned and bailed for that offence. P.C. Hanson, get someone round to Beresford Avenue, check that he's telling the truth?"

"We went there on the way back, Sarge – the old lady had come back with her brother, to pick some bits up. She's going to move in with him, apparently – he lives in Ipswich. She'd found the envelope, and confirmed the amount that Mr. Rockford had said was in it. She'll be coming in tomorrow to square up the paperwork, and collect her property." He nodded at the skull in its evidence bag.

"Good. Right – interview, then."

"Sarge -"

"What?"

"I think he needs a medic, first. He's got injuries which are part of the external factors in the burglary."

"Right. I'll have to call the FME in. Have him wait here. I don't want him in a cell."

"Sarge."

I picked up the phone.

"Hi, it's Sergeant Gardner, Lothing police station – we've got a prisoner with some existing injuries that may be related to another case. Are you able to come and give him the once over? Great – see you shortly."

I looked up as I replaced the phone. "Doctor'll be here in twenty minutes. You're lucky – she's visiting her mother who lives in town. It would've been an hour, otherwise."

I sat back down, and began filing paperwork. The clock on the wall ticked slowly. It was just after six-thirty.

P.C. Tony Raglan
LB 265

"Feroc – Max."

I stared at the two men, trying to work out how I felt about them both being in the same room at the same time. Trying to work out how I felt about Max obviously having been arrested.

"Max has confessed to the Beresford Avenue break-in. He's also returned the money, the other property will be being picked up in the morning."

"Right. So why's he still here? Shouldn't he have been cautioned and released?"

"Helping with enquiries."

"Then why isn't he in interview?"

"Waiting for the doc. I think Max is finally ready to be honest about how he got his injuries."

I raised an eyebrow. "I never did believe you fell down a flight of stairs. And I'm guessing you know damn well our doc won't, once she sees what's happened to you."

Max shook his head.

"So, what did happen?"

"Tony – you know the rules. No talking to the prisoner until he's been interviewed. And especially not in you case. Conflict of interest."

"Sorry Sarge."

I turned to Feroc. "I'll wait for you in the canteen. Apparently Clifford-Alistair wants a brief, so Roscoe can't interview him until the morning now. He told me to pack it in and head home."

Feroc smiled. "Well, do that, then. I could be a while here. I know the way home by now."

"You'll want a lift, though."

"It's only about half an hour's walk."

"Closer to three quarters. And it's dark."

"I'll be fine."

"You'll get a cab."

"Alright, I'll get a cab. Go. I'll be fine."

"You're sure?"

"Tony..."

I held up my hands. "Alright, alright. I'm going. Okay? I'll see you later."

"Yep."

I turned to Max. "You – whatever trouble you've got yourself into, get out of it. Pronto. And think about how you can avoid it the next time."

"I didn't realise it was trouble, not at first."

I sighed. "Save it for the interview. You got a brief?"

"Don't need one. Do I?"

"I don't know – do you?"

"I'm just going to tell them what happened. Everything. Even what I was involved with. How I was involved."

"You know you're entitled to not incriminate yourself?"

"I know, but Alexander'll drag it all up. It'll look better for me if I've told you off my own bat, won't it?"

I sighed again, feeling exhausted. "Yeah. It will."

The door swung open, and a tall, purposeful blonde strode in, a weary smile on her face. I turned to Aimee Gardner. "Looks like the doc's here."

I went out the same door she'd come in, suddenly feeling that I didn't have the words to deal with Max, or Feroc, any more tonight.

Max

The woman – the doctor, apparently – turned to me. "Max Rockford?"

"Yep."

"Come through. Officer, I'm assuming you'll be accompanying him?"

"If that's alright?"

"Of course. I notice he's not in handcuffs."

"No," Feroc answered. "Not that type of night, not for this one."

"Well, at least I won't be covering up for police wrongdoing tonight." She laughed. Feroc echoed her, a little awkwardly. I judged it best to keep my mouth shut.

 The medical room was just like I remembered such places being from school: small, yellowish, with that weird kind of papery stuff on the bed. They had it in tattoo studios, too. Although, thinking about it, my school had had sheets with faded, multi-coloured stripes on. This room, like that long-ago school nurse's office, still smelled of sick overlaid with Dettol.

 "If you'd like to take your shirt off for me. Oh, yes – you've clearly been set about by someone with heavy boots and a grudge, Four, five days ago, maybe?" I nodded. "Any other injuries?"

"No. The kicking was enough."

She ran her hands over my ribs and back. I winced a couple of times, which caused her to pause, and press harder. Finally, she looked up, taking her hands away. "You can put your shirt back on, now." She turned to Feroc. "Nothing broken, amazingly. He'll be sore for a couple of weeks yet, but there's no reason he can't be interviewed."

"Great."

She looked at me again. "If I were you, I'd tell the officers who interview you everything. It might mean you get a chance to get out of the way of the kind of people who do this sort of thing."

"Oh, don't worry – I intend to."

"Good." She smiled. "Unlike many people I end up talking to, you have intelligence. I wish you well."

We left the medical room, and I followed Feroc past the desk
where I'd been signed in, through a set of double doors, to the
kind of interview room that you see on TV cop shows, all despair
and intimidation, watched over by the lazy eye of Big Brother.
The officer who'd driven us back was already waiting, sitting in a
padded chair on one side of the large table. Feroc Hanson sat
down next to him, and I dragged back one of the plastic chairs on
the opposite side of the table.

"Can I get you anything before we start? Glass of water, maybe?"

"No, I'm fine. Let's just get this over with, shall we?"

"Okay. This interview is being recorded, you have the right to
remain silent, but anything you do say can be used against you in
Court. You have the right to stop the interview at any point to
request legal representation. If you become unwell during the
interview, you can request that the interview is paused. An officer
will escort you to the medical bay, where, if necessary, you will be
given appropriate treatment. Do you understand?" I nodded, then
remembered it was being recorded. "Yes. But I should be fine.
And I don't need a solicitor."

"Okay. I will remind you, you can change your mind at any time.
This interview is taking place at seven p.m, on the eleventh of
October, with Maximillian Rockford, known as Max. Officers
present are myself, P.C. Hanson, and P.C. Davis. So, Max – the
doctor has examined some bruises you had when you came in –
do you want to talk to us about how you came by those bruises?"
I swallowed, and took a deep breath.

"I was assaulted by a man who broke in to my boat, the *Kahlo
Dahli*. He had wanted money, money that, in anticipation of his
visit, I had stolen during a break-in at 87 Beresford Avenue.
However, I felt remorse over the break-in almost immediately, and
had already decided I would return the money to the person I had
stolen it from when the man arrived at my boat, expecting me to
hand it over to him. When I told him I didn't have it, he became
violent."

"Do you know this man?"

"Yes. His name's Andrew Parker-James. He works for another

man, a Mr. Alexander Clifford-Alistair."

"And how do you know Mr. Clifford-Alistair?"

I paused, closed my eyes, and took a deep breath. "He recruited me to be part of an investment scheme his company intended to run, under the brand name 'Avin' an Art Attack. It seemed like a good, legitimate investment proposal, at first."

"At first?"

"Yes. It...became apparent that things...weren't quite as they should be. I should have informed the police then, but I was afraid I'd end up being sent to jail for my involvement. And, I suppose, I sort of hoped that I was wrong, that I'd misinterpreted things."

"So, what was the premise of this scheme?"

"Well, Eastern Rise Investments – that's Alexander Clifford-Alistair's company – used the money invested in 'Avin' an Art Attack to offer long-term loans to emerging artists. The idea was that there would be monthly repayments, of which Mr. Clifford-Alistair would keep a percentage, and a percentage would be returned to the initial investment fund. At the end of the investment term, which was a minimum of ten years, the artists were expected to be making regular, significant profit from their work, and were to pay fifty percent of that year's profit to Eastern Rise Investments. Twenty percent would be kept by Eastern Rise, and the remaining eighty would be returned to the original investor."

"Were you one of the artists given loans?"

"No."

"Then how did you come to be involved?"

"The emerging artists – those receiving the loans – were paired with a more established artist. We were given a percentage of the monthly repayments on the loan. It was our job to, well, to bail the artists in receipt of the loans out, should they become unable to repay them."

"And the artist you were assigned to defaulted, leaving you with debts payable to Eastern Rise Investments?"

"Yes. Things haven't been great for me, recently, so I asked for an extension on the due date. Trouble was, I'd already had to ask for one before. I'd managed to make the payment out of my own income, that time, two weeks late. I wasn't offered the same grace this time around. I was told to find the money, anyway I could, or there'd be trouble. I happened to have been visiting a friend in Beresford Avenue, I'd gone to the corner shop there, I heard the woman whose house I later broke into talking about the money she kept in the kitchen... It wasn't really premeditated, as such."

"But you didn't break in immediately."

"No. I was trying to sell some paintings, to earn the money legitimately. But, well, with the economy the way it is, no one was interested. I didn't have a choice."

I sighed, and dropped my head. "No. That's not true. I did have a choice. I could have gone to the police about what was going on."

"What made you think there was a problem, that things weren't quite above board?"

"Gemma – the artist I'd been assigned to, Gemma Radley – told me she'd had her repayments put up. But I happened to know one of the investors, Brynn Ravenswood, through the gallery she works for – she attended an exhibition I was involved with a couple of years ago. I mentioned, in passing, that she must be pleased that her monthly returns had gone up, and – well, she wasn't aware they had. She showed me her paperwork relating to the scheme, and it turned out Eastern Rise had only been registering a quarter of the monthly payments that I knew Gemma had been making. I spoke to some of the other artists – they're all profiled on the website, it's public knowledge who they are, and I knew several of them personally – and it was the same story: there was a massive discrepancy between what they were paying Eastern Rise each month, and what Eastern Rise were recording in their paperwork."

I looked up. "I didn't mean to get involved in anything illegal, you know? I thought I was doing the right thing. I thought I was helping people who needed it."

"I understand, Mr. Rockford. Can you tell us when you first became acquainted with Mr. Clifford-Alistair, and the 'Avin' an Art Attack scheme? Did he approach you, or did you have to apply, how did it work?"

"He approached me. I was flattered. I suppose that's why I didn't look into it as closely as I probably should have done. I was pleased to be asked, you know?"

"I can imagine. So, how did he make contact with you, do you remember?"

"He emailed me. I've got a website, social media stuff, all that. He said he'd seen my work at a couple of the more notable exhibitions I've featured in, and had then checked me out on Instagram and Facebook. He thought I'd make an excellent partner. That was the word he used – 'partner.' Of course, when I started to realise what was going on, it took on rather... sinister connotations."

"Sinister in what way?"

"Well... as though he were saying 'You're part of this, now. As much as I am – so don't you go rocking the boat."

"You felt that he was implying you were as guilty of wrongdoing as him?"

"Well – once I became aware of what was going on, that things weren't all they seemed, then yes. Up to that point, I just thought it was a kind of poncy thing – you know, like solicitors sand the like do."

"Did he ever ask you to put up any money directly? Other than guaranteeing the loan for this artist you were paired with, Gemma?"

I shook my head. "No."

"He didn't ask for any proof that you were in a position to guarantee the loan, if it came to that?"

"Well, kind of – he asked to see my past three years' accounts, but that all seemed above board – like he said, he needed to be sure I was as established an artist as my digital presence suggested." I grinned. "It's ridiculously easy to lie online, you know? So many people see a good quality website – which, let's face it, you can set up for under fifty quid, these days – and assume the person behind it's on the up and up."

"How long have you been working as an artist?"

"If by 'working', you mean 'being paid enough to be charged

income tax', then seven years. I've been selling my work since I was eighteen, though." I laughed. "I made up my mind fairly early on that I didn't fancy traditional employment, although I have tried it. Mellowed a little in my old age. I didn't suit it, and it didn't suit me. My way's harder, less certain, but at least I'm in control of it."

"I can understand that. Do you make much money from your work?"

"Enough. Less than you, probably, but more than some poor sod on minimum wage. I don't have many needs – the *Kahlo Dali*'s brought and paid for, as of four years ago, and the flat in Norwich is fairly cheap. It's not in one of the nice areas, but I don't bother about that. Otherwise, my life is books, music, and art. Norwich has a lot of gigs I can get to free or cheap, a fairly decent library, and lots of charity shops and second hand bookshops, plus the market. And there's Magdalene Street, Anglia Square, and St. Benedict's Street. My manor, if you like. I've got everything I need, fairly close by. My life is relatively simple."

"You've not been involved in criminal enterprises before?"

I licked my lips. "I've been in a bit of trouble, yes. But not for monetary gain. I... I don't know. It was part of a lifestyle, I suppose. Everyone I knew, from the art scene, was all into 'rage against the system, smash the Establishment' – I kind of got carried along. I never did anything actually bad. The burglary, that's the worst thing I've done in my life."

"And you've made restitution for that."

"Yeah." I shrugged. "I'm not really cut out for crime, either, am I?" I sighed, and shook my head. "No good at regular employment. No good at crime. Can't even bring the right kind of flowers to a hospital."

The other copper – Davis? - glanced at Feroc, clearly puzzled. I chuckled. "Sorry. Personal joke."

"Right."

"I'm an artist because I can't really make anything else work, I suppose. But Clifford-Alistair isn't a friend to artists. He's a con artist. And I'll do anything I can to help him get sent down for this.

Do you need Gemma's details?"

Feroc nodded. "If you have them, yes. We'll need to confirm everything with her."

"I feel bad for her, you know? She's genuinely talented. A bit shy, too wary of people thinking she's getting above herself. Lacks confidence, not talent, nor ability."

Feroc studied me. "I'm sure you can help her still – though perhaps not in the way she imagined she would be helped by the 'Avin' an Art Attack scheme."

I nodded slowly. "At the end of the day, I think artists produce better work when we're solely responsible for making our own money."

"I'd agree." Feroc watched me across the table, his eyes as unreadable as Tony's used to be. As Tony's probably still were. I felt suddenly bereft at the thought that I'd never look into those eyes again. Those eyes, that had appeared in so many forms, always devoid from a face, in so many of my paintings. "Do you have Gemma's details?"

"Sorry. Yes." I rummaged in my pocket, and handed over a battered business card. I should have taken better care of it – Gemma made her business cards herself, in the shape of a lotus flower, with gold-etched calligraphic script. It was better than anything I could have produced. As I'd already observed, Gemma wasn't short of talent.

"Thanks. Did she make this herself?"

"Yes. She makes all her business cards. Lotus flowers, hummingbirds, and flared suns. She does them to commission, too."

"This is good. You weren't wrong about her having talent. I'm surprised she felt she needed a loan."

"Everyone needs money, or thinks they do, officer. It's the modern curse. Although, really, it probably isn't all that modern."

Feroc shook his head. "It isn't. So, you admit that you forced entry to, and proceeded to remove items unlawfully from, the premises at eight-seven Beresford Avenue, on the 8th of October this year?"

"Yes."

"Okay, well, I'll take a formal statement about that, and you'll receive an official caution, which will go on your permanent record, and then we'll come back to Alexander Clifford-Alistair, and the full history of your involvement with him."

"Okay."

"We should be done in a couple of hours. I can arrange for someone to run you back to your boat, once we're done?"

"Thanks, but I don't mind walking."

"It's already dark."

"I've walked later at night, and later in the year, than this. The dark half of the year appeals far more to me than spring or summer."

Feroc smiled. I knew he wanted to say what he couldn't, in this formal setting, that Tony was the same. Although Tony preferred autumn, the sense of things changing. My season was winter, when all was sleep, dreams, and potential as yet unrealised. I found it a peaceful season, and one in which I worked well. It had always been my habit to work through the winter, and then slack off, and just attend festivals, fayres, and exhibitions through spring and summer. October was usually dedicated to working on my Christmas pieces – handmade baubles and cards, the odd commission that was being given as a gift.

Feroc stood up. "Okay, if you'll wait here, I'll go and get the statement forms. P.C. Davis'll keep you company." He switched off the taped recording – or was it CD, now? - but I noticed that the CCTV was still on.

 The door closed behind Feroc, and I stretched, and glanced around the room.

"You can stretch your legs, if you like." Davis sounded bored, but not unfriendly.

"Cheers." I got up, and circled the room a couple of times, pausing to do half-press ups against the back wall. I could feel Davis watching me.

"So, how'd you meet Tony Raglan, then?"

I grinned. "Ah, that's a long story. And it belongs in the past, really. If he wants to tell you, he will do."

"No one had a clue, y'know? About him, I mean."

"Most people don't know what's going on in other peoples' heads. It's why they're so fascinating."

"You paint people, then?"

I shook my head. "No. Abstracts. Half-seen things."

"I don't like abstracts much."

A lot of people said that, or something very like it. I liked the fact that the 21st century allowed me to have an answer ready.

"Got a smartphone?"

"Of course." He took it out without waiting to be asked. Most people do that – with phones, with lighters, with business cards. I'd been toying with ideas for a painting on that theme for a few months, but I couldn't pin it down to anything precise.

I handed over one of my own business cards. "That's my website, Instagram, Facebook. Twitter and LinkdIn, too, but they're less relevant. Go to the website first, then check out Instagram. There's a link on the site."

He did as I asked, without question – I learned the art of getting people to thoughtlessly obey from Tony, and I'd learned it well.

"These are actually quite good. I'd always thought of abstracts as stuff a five year old could do, with a crazy price tag slapped on."

"Most people do. And some really simple-looking work takes a lot of practice to make perfect."

The door opened, and Feroc returned. Davis hurriedly put his phone away. I grinned at Feroc, and resumed my seat.

"Right. Burglary first." Feroc switched the tape back on, and ran through the formalities. "Talk me through the burglary, from start to finish. Start with when you first decided to break in to 87 Beresford Avenue, and what motivated you to consider burglary to begin with. I'll write down what you tell me, and you'll have an opportunity to read it through before I ask you to sign it. Okay?"

"Yeah." I felt suddenly nervous. "Let's get this over with."

Alexander

The sound of keys and footsteps. The hatch opening.
"Stand up."
The door opened. David Marchant stepped in to the cell. "Leave the door open, Constable."
"As you wish."
"And give us some privacy?"
The constable glanced back at the black sergeant, who'd clearly accompanied him. She nodded. "Wait just beside the doors. He can't go anywhere, and I don't think he's about to harm Mr. Marchant. He seemed so very keen to see him."
"Sarge." David watched them leave, then turned to me.
"What the hell's going on, Alex?"
"Nothing. It's a misunderstanding, that's all."
"Alex, let's get one thing straight: respectable, responsible citizens do not get arrested for misunderstandings. Okay? Now, what have they arrested you for?"
"They're claiming embezzlement, but, to be honest, I don't think they know."
"They don't have to, at this point. The CPS, potentially the FCA, will clarify the precise charge for them before the case is presented."
"Presented? David – I'm not going to Court over this, am I?"
"You may very well be, Alex. People are very hot about financial crime these days, ever since 2008."
"Look, they've got nothing on me."
"Are you sure about that?"
"Yes. The only people who can give them anything won't. They're as caught up in this as I am."
David looked at me, and I was chilled by what I saw in his eyes.
"Are you certain about that, Alex? Are you absolutely sure?"
"They took money from me, David!"
He shook his head. "That doesn't necessarily implicate them in anything criminal." I lowered my head.

"Oh, hell..."

"Look, Alex, I can help you, but only if you let me. You have to tell me everything, from the very beginning. Leave nothing out."

I looked up.

"Can you make a call for me?"

"I should be able to, yes."

"My mobile – the sergeant took it. There's a number on there, stored as M. R. Mister. Like the title. Call that number, and ask the man who'll answer if he's spoken to the police yet."

"Okay. Is this relevant?"

"It may be."

"I shouldn't really interfere in a police investigation -"

"David, I'm paying you. And paying you quite well, I'd hasten to add. One phone call."

"I'll see what I can do." He stepped into the doorway, raised his voice, and called "Sergeant Gardner!"

The constable opened the door. "Finished already, sir?"

"Not quite. My client has asked me to contact someone on his behalf. I'll need access to his mobile phone."

The constable came up to the cell, motioned Marchant out, and slammed and locked the door behind him. "Let's see what the sergeant has to say about that, shall we?"

Ten minutes later, Marchant was led back to the cell. His face was grim.

"The man who answered the phone – 'MR' , as you call him – answered as he was leaving this station. He walked right past me. And he seemed to know why I was calling. He didn't look nervous at all."

I groaned. If they had Max...

"I think you need to tell me exactly what's going on here, don't you?"

P.C. Tony Raglan
LB 265

I glanced up from the programme I hadn't really been watching as I heard the door open. I could smell Chinese.

Feroc stepped into the room, and held up the thick white carrier bag. "Thought you might be peckish, " he grinned.

"Have I told you I love you recently?"

"Only when I have food."

"Yeah, well, I *really* love you then. But I do love you generally."

I got up, and followed Feroc through to the kitchen, pausing to get a couple of beers out of the fridge. "So – what happened? What did Max have to say?"

Feroc grinned. "Quite a lot, as it happens." He glanced at the beers. "I think you might want to put those back – tonight's more a gin and pineapple night, I think.

"That good?"

"If the CPS don't screw it up, and Clifford-Alistair doesn't try and get clever tomorrow morning. But he's being charged, no question. The evidence Max gave?" He shook his head. "He's not getting out of it. And we've got a couple of other artists who were caught up in this scheme coming in tomorrow to make their own statements. It won't just be Max's word against Clifford-Alistair's."

"Good. That's definitely worth drinking to." I paused, the bottle of gin halfway out of the fridge. "Hang on. I need to change my shirt."

"What?"

"Yeah – if we're celebrating, I feel I should put on a clean shirt. You plate up – I'll be back in a sec."

"Shall I sort the drinks out?"

"Nah, I'll do that. You'll only put too much pineapple or too much gin in."

When I came back, it was with one hand behind my back. I dropped to one knee, brought my hand out in front of me. Two wedding rings, inscribed with runic script, were tied to a bottle of champagne.

"Tony – what the -"

"Feroc...think very carefully before you answer, because this is possibly the most important question I'm ever going to ask you: Will you marry me?"

I couldn't look at him. I focused on the champers, instead, feeling my sweat start to cling to the bottle, watching the glint of the reflection of the rings.

Silence can be deafening, sometimes.

Suddenly, into that silence like a feather dropped into the Grand Canyon, came Feroc's answer.

"Yes."

It was as terrifying and as beautiful, as complicatedly simple, as that. It always had been.

Printed in Great Britain
by Amazon